PUFF

DREA

Claire and her parents ha~~ve recently moved into a cr~~ambling sixteenth-century country house. The locals call it 'bad luck house', but they find it a warm and welcoming place – all except for Claire's bedroom which is cold and frightening. Even the cat is afraid of the atmosphere pervading the room. That night, Claire has a dream that is to haunt her: of a boy holding a sparkling necklace and appearing to plead with her for help. As Claire begins to uncover the buried history of the house, she realizes that she must recover the necklace to free the house from its shadows. But it soon becomes a race against time as the mysterious and menacing Jeremy Knight seems to be seeking the same prize and will stop at nothing to win it. A compelling story of greed, obsession and tragedy with a heart-stopping climax.

Rosemary Hayes has worked in advertising, marketing and publishing. In 1987 her first children's novel *Race Against Time* was runner up for the Kathleen Fidler Award and since then she has written regularly for children. She runs a small publishing house in rural Cambridgeshire where she lives with her husband, their three children and an assortment of unruly animals.

*Also by Rosemary Hayes*

**THE GREMLIN BUSTER
RACE AGAINST TIME**

# DREAMCHILD

## ROSEMARY HAYES

PUFFIN BOOKS

PUFFIN BOOKS

Published by the Penguin Group
Penguin Books Ltd, 27 Wrights Lane, London W8 5TZ, England
Penguin Books USA Inc., 375 Hudson Street, New York, New York 10014, USA
Penguin Books Australia Ltd, Ringwood, Victoria, Australia
Penguin Books Canada Ltd, 10 Alcorn Avenue, Toronto, Ontario, Canada M4V 3B2
Penguin Books (NZ) Ltd, 182–190 Wairau Road, Auckland 10, New Zealand

Penguin Books Ltd, Registered Offices: Harmondsworth, Middlesex, England

First published by Blackie and Son Ltd 1990
Published in Puffin Books 1992
1 3 5 7 9 10 8 6 4 2

# Chapter One

Claire stood in her bedroom and looked about her. The bookshelves and chest-of-drawers were empty and the rugs had been rolled up and stacked in the corner. All the pictures had been taken off the walls leaving lighter patches on the wallpaper where they had hung. Claire remembered choosing the wallpaper and she touched it gently, tracing the pattern with her finger. Then she picked up her old teddy from the floor and stuffed him into a plastic bag with some other bits and pieces. She wasn't sorry to be leaving. The bare room had lost its character and already she was thinking about what lay ahead – a new house, new friends and a new school. She shivered, half excited, half frightened.

All her life, Claire had lived in the same house in the same town and now suddenly everything was changing. They were leaving to go and live miles away in a tumble-down house out in the country.

Her friends had crowded round her at school when she'd shown them photos.

'It looks great! Can we come and stay in the holidays?'

'Look at all those fields!'

'Won't you feel spooky with no other houses around?'

Claire had hugged the photos to her, smiling at the circle of familiar faces. 'Mum says you can *all* come and stay as soon as we've got straight. There's loads of room.'

Her mother's voice drifted up from downstairs, breaking into her thoughts. 'Hurry up, Claire, the removal people are arriving. Have you finished yet?'

Claire looked out of the window. She watched as the huge removal van crawled up the street while the driver checked the numbers on the doors. At last the van shuddered to a stop outside their front garden.

Slinging the plastic bag over her shoulder, Claire clumped down the stairs two at a time and almost collided with her mother who was at the bottom, piling up things in the hall.

'Hey. Watch it!' said Mum, laughing.

Claire added her stuff to the pile and then took a heavy load from her mother's arms. Mum was expecting a baby. At last, there was to be another member of the family, and every time she thought about it, Claire couldn't stop a smile bubbling up from the happiness deep inside her. She'd always wanted a brother or sister and now, after years of waiting, it was to happen. In fact everything was happening at once!

Claire glanced at her mum. Although her face was content, her eyes were tired. For the first time Claire realised, with a shock, how strained she looked, behind her cheerful exterior. Mum was supposed to be taking it easy and this move was tiring her out.

'Go and sit down for a bit Mum,' said Claire.

'Oh, don't fuss. I'm fine,' said Mum, but she did go into the kitchen and sit down at the table to write out the last of the labels to stick on the furniture. Most of it had already gone and the rest would go today.

There was a ring at the door, and, a few moments later, Claire's dad came into the kitchen followed by the removal men. He put his hands on his wife's shoulders and smiled at Claire over her head. 'Any chance of a cup of tea?'

Claire was glad to have something to do. She busied herself making tea for everyone and when she handed a cup to her father, he drew her aside. 'Try and make sure Mum keeps quiet,' he said. 'There's nothing else she needs to do now and we've still got a long journey ahead of us.'

As the removal men set to work upstairs, Claire sat down beside her mum.

'Tell me about the house again,' she said.

Mum laughed. 'You'll see for yourself soon.'

'But I want to imagine it. Then see if it's like I've imagined.'

Mum sat back in her chair and clasped her hands behind her head. 'Well . . . it's very old. Parts go back to the 16th Century apparently. It stands by itself on top of a hill some way outside a small market town.'

'Yes, I know all that. I've seen the photos. But I want to know about the inside.'

Mum frowned. She sat up, unclasped her hands and took a gulp of tea. 'I hope you won't find it too draughty and old-fashioned. It hasn't been lived in for several years and there's an awful lot that needs doing to it. There's no central heating, for a start.'

Claire made a face. 'Well, at least it's summer.'

Mum smiled. 'I'm sure you'll love it. The kitchen's huge, with these wonderful oak beams, and there are big open fireplaces in most of the rooms. And the view is fantastic, especially from your bedroom. You can look right out over the fields to the river.'

Mum went on. 'I wish you could have come with us when we went to see it. But it was all such a rush.'

Claire nodded. Her dad had been wanting to get out of his job in the city for a long time and suddenly he'd got the chance to buy into this run-down factory. Dad had explained that the factory gave jobs to almost half the local people and if it closed, hundreds of people would be out of work. He was sure he could make it profitable again and it was just the sort of challenge he'd always wanted.

The last few weeks had been hectic. The new house was nearly two hundred miles away, somewhere in the West Country. Mum and Dad had travelled down there several times to meet people at the factory and to look for somewhere to live, but Claire had been in the middle of school exams, so she hadn't gone with them.

'There's this funny old back staircase that goes up to your bedroom,' said Mum. 'It's sort of secret because it's behind doors either end and, if you didn't know, you'd think it was just a cupboard. It's so steep I don't suppose we'll ever use it, but it's very old and the wood is worn in the middle of every step. Hundreds of people must have run up and down over the years.'

Mum put down her cup and folded her arms. 'What else can I tell you? Oh yes. Some of the doorways are so low that you have to duck before you go into the room.'

'Why are they so low?'

'Because people used to be much smaller, I suppose!'

Claire looked at her mother's face, alight with excitement.

'You really like the house, don't you?'

Mum nodded. 'As soon as we saw it, both Dad and I knew we wanted to live there.' She made a face and shifted in her chair, her body awkward with the weight of the baby. 'Though I think we're a bit mad, too. There's so much work to be done on the place.'

Claire looked out of the kitchen window. The removal men had got into a steady rhythm and, slowly but surely, the house was being emptied into the van. It was funny to think of their possessions travelling by road from one house to the other.

At last the van drove away, lumbering through the gears up the street. Claire and her parents stood at the front door and watched until it turned the corner out of sight. Other people in the street were watching, too, and several neighbours crowded round their car as Dad loaded up the last bits and pieces, Mum checked all the windows and doors, and Claire went looking for the cat.

'Come on, Dodo,' she called 'I know you're here somewhere.' Claire searched the house and then the garden and finally the house again.

Dodo (his real name was Orlando) was a large ginger tomcat and he didn't think much of all this coming and going and furniture shifting. Even his basket had disappeared. When his hiding place was finally discovered (deep in a dark corner of a kitchen cupboard) he looked accusingly at Claire.

She laughed at his outraged expression. 'Come on boy. You'll get left behind.' She picked him up and tried to put him into the special carrier. Dodo fought, kicking out with his back legs. He didn't want to be trapped in a wire basket! Dad came to the rescue and eventually they managed to hold down the heavy, furious mass of ginger hair and sharp claws long enough to secure the catch.

When Dodo had joined the rest of the luggage in the car, Dad started the engine and they turned out of the drive.

A group of their neighbours and some of Claire's school friends were on the pavement outside to wave them off.

'Goodbye! Good luck! We're all going to come and visit!'

Claire leaned out of the window to wave back and to

9

mouth a silent goodbye to their empty house with the 'SOLD' sign outside.

They reached the end of the street and turned on to the main road. The friends and the house disappeared and Claire wound up the window and flopped back in her seat. Soon all the other familiar streets and shops had disappeared, too, and they were heading towards the motorway and their new life.

Claire settled down with Dodo beside her in his basket. She talked to him, tried to stroke him through the bars, and even sang pop songs to him. But he just yowled in time with the engine and refused to be comforted, so, in the end, she stopped trying.

'We'll have a nice lunch at a country pub,' said Mum, turning round to Claire.

Claire grinned and nodded, then she yawned. She tried to read the book she'd brought but the words danced in front of her eyes. At last she gave up and drifted off to sleep, her head lolling on her shoulder.

The car stopped and she woke with a start. She had been dreaming about the new house and the dream had been so vivid that it stayed with her for several minutes after she was awake. In the dream she had seen the house as it must have looked before it was neglected. Its garden was full of flowers and the windows at the front were flung open, welcoming them, inviting them to live in it.

Claire sat up, yawning, and rubbed her aching neck. 'I had a lovely dream,' she said. 'All about the house.'

'Which one?' asked Dad.

'The new one.'

'You mean the old new one?'

Claire smiled, she was used to her father's teasing. 'All right. The new old one,' she said. '*Anyway*,' she went on, 'I dreamt it was all mended and the garden planted with flowers and stuff. It looked really great.'

'Perhaps one day it will again,' said Dad. 'I can see I shall be painting and decorating and mending and digging and weeding for years to come!'

'Some hope!' said Claire and Mum together. It was a family joke that Dad was always *talking* about doing jobs around the house and garden but never actually getting round to *doing* them. Dad always made lots of plans, but it was usually Mum who quietly got on with the work.

Dad made a face. 'You wait!' he muttered. 'I'll show you. I'm going to become a real do-it-yourself man.'

'No!' shouted Mum in mock horror. 'Anything but that. Please!'

'You've got no faith in me, either of you!' said Dad.

Mum patted his back. 'Of course we have! But not as a do-it-yourself man.' She started to giggle. 'Do you remember the kitchen shelves, Claire . . .'

Claire remembered only too well. To this day she could see the herb jars sliding to the end of the gently sloping shelves and crashing to the floor. Dad stood back to admire his handiwork while she and Mum rolled about behind him, helpless with mirth.

'And what about the coffee table!'

Tears of laughter ran down their faces as Claire and Mum relived the birthday when Dad had given Mum a coffee table he'd made himself. It was only when it was standing in the living-room and he had tried to put something on it that he'd realised that one leg was shorter than the others!

Dad pretended to sulk for a few seconds but he couldn't keep it up for long and soon he started to laugh, too. Then he swung off at the next motorway

11

exit and, still laughing, they drove up a side road and stopped outside a country pub.

The weather was unsettled, but as they parked, the sun came out from behind a cloud and they felt its warmth on their backs when they got out of the car and stretched their cramped limbs. Claire took some deep breaths of country air. From now on, it was always going to smell like this – fresh and free from the polluting fumes of traffic. She couldn't wait to get on and see the new house for herself.

After lunch, Mum drove. The miles slipped by and it started to rain again. They listened to cassettes, to the radio, played a few car games and, at last, fell silent.

The rain stopped but it was still overcast.

'Only ten miles from here,' said Mum, and her voice was excited. Claire sat up and looked out of the window as they left the motorway for the last time and drove along country lanes with steep hedgerows on either side. She wound down the window. It was impossible to go fast on these roads and she could smell the freshness of the countryside newly washed by rain. The hedgerows gave way to stone walls, shielding flocks of incurious sheep. Claire trailed her hand out of the car window and let lazy unconnected thoughts drift into her mind.

'It's just round the next corner, Claire,' said Dad. 'It's the house on top of the hill. You'll be able to see it in a minute.'

Claire leaned forward and stared out of the window. The car eased round a sharp bend and there on the right was the hill with a single house standing on top. It was still some way off and nothing could be seen in detail, but immediately, Claire gave a little shiver of excitement.

Her mother stopped the car and they all gazed at the

house in the distance. Dad turned to Claire and smiled at her but he didn't speak.

Claire could understand why her parents wanted to live there. Even from this distance there was something defiant and proud about the place, standing alone, shielded from the elements only by the group of trees behind.

Mum put the car in gear and they moved off again past some cottages and a duck pond then up the hill leading to the house. Claire's heart started to beat faster. At last they reached the top of the hill and drove up to a closed gate which leant drunkenly forward, only held on by one hinge. To one side of the gate, half hidden by an overgrown hedge, was a wooden board, the paint blistered and peeling. Claire could just make out the words on the board 'Stephanie House'. Dad got out of the car and heaved the gate open. As he gave it a last shove to wedge it more firmly, the remaining hinge gave way and the gate fell back into the hedge. He turned to the others and grinned, then he strode on ahead of them up to the house.

Almost before Mum had stopped the car outside the front door Claire was out on the drive. She put her hands in the pockets of her jacket and looked at her new home. Part of it was timbered and part was brick. Some of the guttering was missing and some was hanging uselessly down. The garden was wild and overgrown and nothing had been painted for years. Yet, even in its decrepit state, Claire really liked it. They were right, there was something special about it.

She hugged her parents. 'It's great!' she said. 'I love it!'

Mum rummaged in her bag for the key and unlocked the front door. It creaked as she pushed it open. Inside there was a small hall with a stone floor and from this a beautiful wooden staircase led up to a landing with a huge window which stretched from floor to ceiling.

Claire gasped. 'It's so light! I thought it would be all dark and pokey.'

Mum put her hand on the wooden scroll at the bottom of the banisters. 'I think the staircase is almost the best thing in the house.'

'Wait till you see the other staircase,' said Dad. 'You'd never know it was there unless someone told you. Come on, I'll show you round.' Eagerly he led her through the downstairs rooms – the dining room, the study, the cloakroom with its old-fashioned fittings and then into the kitchen.

'Here's the other staircase,' said Dad.

'Where?' Claire could see nothing.

Dad grinned and opened what looked like an ordinary cupboard set into the wall. Claire peered inside and saw nothing but darkness, then Dad switched on the light to reveal steep wooden steps stretching upwards. Claire ran half-way up, slipping and stumbling, then turned and came back.

'It's weird!'

Mum joined them. 'You haven't seen your room yet. Come on, I'll show you now. Wait till you see the view!'

They went up the front stairs together and Mum led the way along the passage to the room at the end. She flung the door open. 'There!'

The room had a sloping ceiling and big casement window with a seat running along the bottom of it. It faced West and now the afternoon sun flooded in, making patterns on the bare floorboards.

Pausing at the door, Claire was gripped with a sudden unreasonable fear. The room was lovely, it was

14

everything she could have wanted, but she suddenly felt cold and uneasy. She made herself walk into the room, but the feeling wouldn't go away. There was something in the room she didn't like, something that made her frightened, but she couldn't explain what. She shivered and pulled her jacket closely round her.

'Do you like it?' Mum was standing smiling by the window and just for a second, Claire thought someone else was there too – another much shorter woman, wearing a long dress. A woman who was also pregnant. Claire blinked and the image was gone. She shrugged. It must have been a trick of the light.

Claire went over to Mum. She knelt on the window seat and looked out over the fields leading down to the river. 'It's lovely,' she said, then she turned and saw the cupboard door.

'Is this the other end of the staircase?'

Mum nodded, and Claire opened the door and slithered and slipped down the well-worn stairs to the kitchen. Although she couldn't explain why, she didn't want to stay in her bedroom any longer. Perhaps it would be different when her things were all in place.

'I must get Dodo,' she shouted from half-way down.

'Don't forget to butter his paws,' yelled Mum.

Claire turned back when she reached the kitchen. 'What!'

'Butter his paws.' Mum's voice drifted eerily down the stairs. 'Then he'll have to spend a long time cleaning them. By the time he's finished he'll have got used to being here. It's an old trick, but it usually works.'

Buttering Dodo's paws took some time. After his undignified journey in a basket in the car, he was in a foul temper, and when Claire and Dad smeared butter all over his paws, it didn't improve. When they let him

15

out he tried to run off but the desire to lick his sticky paws was greater than the desire to escape and he spent a long time by the kitchen stove licking off the butter before he finally settled down to sleep on top of a pile of tea towels.

It was late in the evening by the time the removal people had been and gone and most of the furniture was in the right place. After supper, Claire couldn't keep her eyes open any longer. She kissed her parents goodnight and headed for bed, only pausing to collect Dodo.

Dodo had always slept in Claire's bedroom, ever since they'd first had him, a tiny ball of ginger fluff with wide green eyes. Claire gathered the sleepy cat, who was past resistance now, and slowly climbed up the stairs.

As she entered her bedroom, she felt the cat struggle in her arms, suddenly awake and kicking against her.

'Don't be silly, Dodo. Your basket's here – look!'

Claire went into her room and closed the door. She carried the cat over to the basket and tried to settle him down. But he refused to get in. His hair stood on end and his eyes were wild. He fled to the door and started to scratch frantically. Claire frowned. Could it be that the cat, too, sensed something odd about this room? She opened the door and watched him bolt down the landing. Then, too tired to worry about it, she turned back into her room and started to get ready for bed.

She should have been warm. She was in her usual bed with her usual bedclothes, yet she was shivering. And after such a long and exhausting day she should have gone to sleep immediately. But she tossed and turned, feeling unhappy in this room. She didn't know

16

why. She felt very happy and at ease everywhere else in the house. It was a welcoming, warm house and she loved it. All except this room. It frightened her and she couldn't understand why.

# Chapter Two

It was a long time before Claire slept and when at last she did, her dreams were frightening – full of strange unconnected images. She woke up in the early hours of the morning, just as dawn was streaking the sky. Drowsily, she reached out and fumbled for her clock which should have been on the table beside her bed. But instead, her hand banged against the wall and it took her a moment to remember that she was in the new house and that nothing was in its usual place. She sat up and hugged her knees. Outside, the birds were beginning their dawn chorus. Claire smiled to herself. The birds must have woken her. They were a lot noisier here. She was about to pull the duvet over her head to drown out the sound when a very slight movement caught her eye and something – the faintest sound like the swish of material – came from near the window. Once again, Claire thought she saw the outline of a figure and she sat bolt upright, her heart pounding.

'Who is it?' she said. She tried to sound brave, but her voice came out as a squeak.

There was no reply and, indeed, if there had been an image, it had melted immediately into the walls.

Claire was wide awake now. She pulled on her dressing-gown and shuffled her feet into her slippers. Cautiously she padded over to the window, sat on the low seat and looked round the room. No one was there. Claire shrugged and told herself not to be stupid. It was a strange house, an old house. It would take time

18

to get used to it. She gazed out of the window. There were no curtains up yet and she watched as gradually the view came into focus and a mist rose from the river and rolled over the fields.

She shivered and rubbed her arms. She felt so cold in this room. She crept out into the passage, her first instinct to go and tell Mum and Dad about her odd experience. But she felt better once she was away from her bedroom so, instead, she tiptoed down the front staircase in the half-light and went into the kitchen. The cat was still sleeping on top of the tea-towels beside the stove, worn out from the effort of removing so much butter from his paws. Claire stroked him but he hardly stirred.

She searched through the packing cases until she found what she wanted, then she made herself a warm drink as the light strengthened and the birdsong became ever more insistent. At last, warmed and relaxed, she went upstairs again. But the moment she walked from the passage into her bedroom she felt the coldness envelop her. It hit her like a physical blow as she walked through the door, yet there was no reason for it. The passage wasn't cold and there weren't any obvious draughts. Yet here, in her new bedroom, the atmosphere was different from anywhere else in the house. It was an atmosphere that made her feel uneasy and restless – and very cold. She frowned and got into bed again. As the countryside was waking up, Claire fell asleep, but she didn't feel rested when her mother finally woke her for breakfast.

Claire dressed quickly and went downstairs. She decided to surpise her parents and use the secret staircase. Mum shrieked and nearly dropped the saucepan she was carrying, and Dodo leapt up from his nest on top of the tea-towels and yowled aggressively as Claire burst through the door into the kitchen.

'Woops! Sorry!' said Claire, grinning. She kissed Mum and went over to comfort Dodo. But he still hadn't forgiven Claire and he stalked away across the kitchen floor and settled down in the far corner to wash.

'Come and have some breakfast love,' said Mum, once she'd recovered from the shock. 'It's like having a picnic. Nothing's in its proper place yet.'

Claire sat down at the table. She felt better after breakfast and last night's feelings about her room didn't seem so important any more. Casually, she said, 'I had a lot of funny dreams last night.' Then, not looking at Mum, she went on, 'And I felt a bit spooky in that room.'

Mum was reading the ads in the local paper. 'I expect you were overtired,' she said, absently. 'It'll take a while to get used to everything here.'

Claire nodded. It all seemed different in the daylight. She put any doubts about her bedroom firmly out of her mind.

Dad came into the room.

'I've been in the fields behind the house,' he said, pulling off his wellingtons and letting them fall beside the stove. 'It's glorious country. You can walk right down to the river from here.'

He put on his shoes, then grabbed a final cup of tea and slurped it down before packing some files into his bulging briefcase. After a brief fight with the catch, he finally got it closed. He kissed Mum and Claire goodbye and headed for the door.

'My first proper day at the factory,' he said. 'Wish me luck.'

20

They watched his car disappear down the hill and then went back into the kitchen to make some plans.

Claire and Mum spent most of the day unpacking and sorting and putting away. Every now and then they would stop and have a break. Once they walked all the way round the garden trying to work out where the flowerbeds had been and what plants were worth saving.

Mum sat down on a rickety garden seat. 'There's so much to do here. I don't know where to begin.'

'Perhaps we could get some help?'

Mum nodded. 'Yes, I think we'll have to have someone in to help get the garden straight.' She frowned. 'But we can't afford much help. Things aren't going to be easy, Claire. We've risked everything to buy into the factory and get this house.'

'Why don't you go and ask, anyway,' said Claire. 'Ask the people who live in the cottages at the bottom of the hill.'

'That's a good idea. We'll go down this evening.'

It was late afternoon by the time they stopped working.

Mum sighed. 'I'm feeling a bit tired. I'll just go and have a rest for half-an-hour then we'll walk down the hill and talk to the people in the cottages.'

Claire watched her mother mount the stairs and saw how she heaved her weight up every step. Claire knew that the doctor had told her to be very careful. She should have had a rest earlier in the day. Claire frowned. She must try and stop Mum doing too much.

She went on with her job, taking books out of boxes and putting them in order on the shelves in the study. She liked the study. They'd never had a study before. It was a small room with an old-fashioned fireplace, lots of bookshelves and a bow window looking out onto

21

the front drive. Claire worked hard, dusting shelves and following the lists that Mum had written so that the books all got put in order. She worked on steadily, humming tunelessly to herself, her thoughts miles away.

It was as she was making one of the many journeys between bookshelves and packing case that she happened to look up and glance out of the window. She was holding a pile of books and she stopped and stood still. There was a man at the entrance to the drive standing in the gap where the gate should have been if Dad hadn't broken it yesterday. The man was looking up at the house and he didn't notice Claire. He was a tall man with dark hair, a rather beaky nose and he was dressed in expensive-looking clothes – clothes which looked out of place deep in the country. For some reason she couldn't explain, Claire felt scared when she saw him, felt somehow as though he was spying on her. She turned back towards the bookshelves again. She knew she was being silly. He had every right to look at the house, didn't he? There was no law against standing in the road looking.

Suddenly the quiet was shattered by a frantic barking followed by fierce growling. Claire dropped the books and ran to the window. From nowhere a dog had appeared and it was flinging itself upon the stranger at the gate. The man was hitting out at the dog, trying to fend it off, but it wouldn't be quieted and at last the man turned away and disappeared into the road. Claire continued to watch as the dog came back through the gateway, sat in a patch of sunlight on the drive, had a lengthy scratch, then yawned and lay down.

Claire had never seen a dog like it before. It was lean and long-legged. There must have been a greyhound somewhere in its family history but it wasn't smooth like a greyhound. It had a broken coat of shaggy golden colour and it seemed quite at home. Claire smiled and went on unpacking the books.

It was early evening by the time Mum came downstairs again. She looked better.

'I must have gone to sleep,' she said as she came downstairs. 'I didn't mean to spend so long up there.'

She stretched and looked round the hall. 'Is Dad back yet?'

Claire shook her head.

'Never mind. We'll leave him a note and we'll go to the cottages. The walk will do us good.'

'Are you sure you can manage?' asked Claire anxiously. 'It's a steep climb back up the hill.'

Mum nodded. 'I'll be fine.'

They went out of the front door into the evening sun. Mum took a deep breath. 'It's so quiet and peaceful,' she said.

'It wasn't earlier on,' said Claire, and she told Mum about the man at the gate and the dog.

'Oh look!' she said, pointing down the drive. 'The dog's still here.'

Cautiously they approached it, but there was no sign of its earlier aggression. It wagged its tail, rolled over and expected its tummy to be tickled. Claire bent down, obligingly tickled the pale yellow-fawn tummy and fondled its silky ears.

'You'd better go home now, boy.'

The dog continued to wag its tail and showed no sign of moving.

'We'll ask where it belongs when we get to the cottages,' said Mum, and they walked out on to the road, leaving the dog on the drive.

The air was heavy with the scent of wildflowers as

they made their way down the hill, and every now and then they caught a glimpse of the river as it wound its way lazily into the distance. It didn't take long to get down and then they turned to the left and walked along the road to the row of cottages they'd passed yesterday.

They went in at the first gate and knocked at a green-painted wooden door. Claire hung back behind her mother and she noticed the twitch of net curtains from another cottage in the row. There was a cough and a shuffling movement from inside, then the door opened and an elderly man peered out. He looked them up and down but said nothing.

Mum cleared her throat. 'We've just moved into Stephanie House,' she said.

'Oh, yes,' said the old man, and a flicker of interest crossed his face.

Mum introduced herself and Claire and the old man nodded.

'Alec Toombs,' he said, extending his hand. He shook Mum's hand up and down, then released it and said, 'My wife used to help up at Stephanie House in the old days.'

Mum said quickly, 'I was wondering if you knew of anyone who might come and help *us*. It's the garden that needs most attention . . .'

Alec nodded. 'I might manage a few hours a week. I can't promise, mind, because my back gives me a bit of trouble these days. I'll have a word with the wife and see what she says. She might do a few hours in the house for you, too.'

Mum smiled. 'We'd be really grateful,' she said.

They chatted on for a while. Mum asked where she should go for this and that, who might come and mend the gutter and so on. Alec Toombs rubbed his chin and gave slow but thoughtful answers.

24

Just as they were leaving, Claire spoke. 'There's a dog up at the house – a sort of greyhound with a rough coat. Do you know who it belongs to?'

'No one round here,' said Alec. 'I've never seen a dog like that round here.'

'Oh, well,' said Mum. 'I expect it will find its way home.'

They said goodbye to Alec and as they turned to walk up the path to the gate he said, 'Are you staying long then?'

Mum frowned, wondering what he meant. 'At the house? Yes, I hope so. My husband's job has brought us here. I hope we'll stay a very long time.'

Alec grunted. 'There's been nothing but changes up at that house. People come then the next minute you hear they've gone away again. No one stays for long.'

Mum and Claire didn't speak as they climbed up the hill. Mum had to stop often to rest and it took them a long time to get back. When at last they reached the house, Claire thought at first that the dog had gone – there was no sign of him in the drive – and she felt a pang of disappointment. But as they reached the front door, they found him lying, fast asleep, in the porch. He got to his feet, stretched and wagged his tail. Then, as Mum put the key in the lock and opened the door, he pushed his way into the hall and padded straight into the kitchen.

Unfortunately the dog reached the kitchen before Claire and there was an outraged yowl and the sound of something crashing to the floor. Claire ran in and saw Dodo perched on top of the dresser, his fur erect like a ginger bottle-brush, glaring down at the intruder. Several plates on the dresser had crashed to the ground and the dog was wagging its tail, licking hopefully at the broken china, oblivious to the cat's fury.

Dad was in the kitchen, too. He had just arrived and had been reading the note they'd left him when the explosion of dog and cat had whirled round his feet.

'What's *that*!' he shouted, pulling a horrified face and pointing at the dog.

Claire rushed over to Dodo and tried to calm him down. 'I don't know. He just turned up. No one seems to know where he belongs.'

As if on cue, the dog left the broken plates and jumped up, put its paws on Dad's chest and tried to lick his hand. Dad smiled and pushed it away. 'Not on my office suit. Get down!'

Dodo, who was now in Claire's arms, looked disgusted.

Mum came in and sat down. She burst out laughing when she saw the cat's expression.

'Poor Dodo. He looks really offended. We'll have to find the dog's owners.'

Dad put on the kettle, then he took off his jacket, loosened his tie and sat down at the kitchen table. He stretched his arms high above his head. 'It's great to be able to get home from work in just a few minutes.'

'No more buses or trains,' said Mum. Then she went on, 'How did it go – your first proper day?'

There was the smallest hesitation before he replied, '. . . Oh, fine.'

Mum picked up the hesitation immediately. She unearthed a bottle of whisky from a packing case and poured him a stiff drink. As she handed it to him, she said, frowning, 'Are you sure everything's all right?'

Dad took the drink gratefully and had an appreciative sip. Then he shrugged and bent to stroke the dog. 'Yes. Yes, I think so. It's just that somehow the atmosphere at the factory seemed to have changed since I was there last week.'

'What do you mean?'

'Well, last time I was there, everyone was really friendly. They couldn't wait for me to come and start work. Yet today, they were all very polite but suspicious, somehow. I can't really explain, but I certainly sensed it.'

'Don't be ridiculous!' said Mum. 'You're just tired. It'll all seem different in the morning.'

'Yes, I expect you're right.' Dad stretched again. Then he took the dog's head between his hands and addressed it:

'Seeing as you're here, dog,' he said, 'you can come out with me for an evening walk.'

# Chapter Three

'That dog must go!' said Mum.

'What's he done now?' asked Claire, coming into the kitchen. Then she started to laugh. Everything that had been on the table was on the floor, everything edible had been eaten, the cat's dish had been polished clean and the dog was lying in a patch of evening sunlight on the floor, fast asleep.

'I expect he was hungry,' said Claire, bending down to stroke him.

'He must go. He's not ours and he doesn't belong here,' said Mum.

'*He* thinks he belongs here! Oh please don't turn him out, Mum. Let him stay – just for tonight. I'll look after him.'

Mum sighed. 'Just for tonight, then. Tomorrow we'll take him to the police station.'

When Claire went up to bed that night, the dog followed her. He bounded up the stairs and pushed ahead of her into her bedroom, apparently knowing exactly where to go. He jumped up onto the bed and settled comfortably at the end, his paw over his nose and his eyes on Claire, silently begging her not to turn him out.

She smiled and stroked him and his tail beat on the duvet. *He* was certainly not spooked by anything in the room.

'You are a very bad dog,' said Claire, as she got ready for bed. 'You are taking over the house.' But she smiled as she said it and secretly she was very glad to have him with her. She crawled into bed, feeling his comforting warmth at her feet, and was soon asleep.

That night she had the first of many dreams she was to have about the boy. It was very vivid, unlike any dream she'd ever had before.

The boy was about her own age and was standing by a tree-stump beside a river. He was dressed in old-fashioned clothes, clothes from another age, and in his outstretched hand he held a beautiful necklace of precious stones. He seemed to be trying to tell Claire something, but she couldn't understand what he was saying.

In the morning, she could still remember the dream very clearly. She could picture the boy with his anxious expression and outstretched hand and see the exact place where he stood, at a bend in a river, by an old tree-stump.

At breakfast, Claire told Mum about the dream but again, in daylight it seemed unimportant. And in any case, Mum had something else on her mind. 'I took Dad to the office earlier,' she said firmly. 'So we've got the car today and the first thing we must do is to take that dog to the police.'

Claire pleaded but it was no use.

'He's sure to belong to someone, love. Some child is probably missing him terribly. We must tell the police we've got him.'

The dog leapt trustingly into the back of the car and they set off for the town. Claire sat beside him, stroking his nose and praying that no one had reported him missing.

The town wasn't very big and the police station was in the main street. The policeman on duty looked in the record book but it seemed that no one had reported a missing dog. He peered down at the dog and scratched his chin. 'I've never seen it round here before. It's a funny looking dog, isn't it? Not the sort of dog you'd forget in a hurry.'

Mum smiled and looked down at the rangy frame and melting brown eyes. 'No, he's certainly unusual!'

Claire tugged at her sleeve. 'Oh, *please* can we keep him Mum? I'll look after him, I promise. I'll take him for walks and feed him and everything.'

Mum hesitated and the dog thrust its nose into her hand.

'Please!' said Claire.

Mum sighed. 'Oh, all right. But only until we can find the owners.'

Claire smiled and squatted down beside the dog. She gave him a hug and he returned her affection with some enthusiastic licking.

They put the dog in the back of the car then strolled down the main street of the town. They peered into shop windows and looked around them at the old half-timbered buildings tucked between the newer shops and offices.

'Look at that!' said Mum. They had stopped outside a fine Tudor building which stood on its own in a courtyard spilling over with flowers.

'Oh, it's the museum,' said Mum. 'Let's go and look round.'

Claire yawned. She didn't want to be dragged round a museum. She wanted to get back to the house. She was just about to protest when she suddenly had an idea.

'Do you think they'd have any stuff about Stephanie House in the museum?'

Mum looked interested. 'Umm, I don't know. But we can ask.'

They went in through a heavy oak door, studded with nails. The man at the kiosk was reading a newspaper and he tore off some tickets and handed them to Mum without looking at her.

'I want to find out about a house near here,' she said.

'Oh, yes,' said the man. He didn't sound at all interested.

'It's very old. It's called Stephanie House.'

Suddenly the man's head shot up.

'Stephanie House? Are you living there, then?'

'Yes,' said Mum. 'We've just moved in.'

The man said no more but Claire felt as though he was about to tell them something and then thought better of it. Instead, he put down his paper and pressed a button on his telephone. 'Mr Harris can probably help you. He's the curator. I'll see if he's about.'

He spoke on the phone then turned back to them. 'He's got a meeting soon but you could see him for a few minutes.' The man showed them where to go and then went back to reading his newspaper.

Claire and Mum walked through several rooms full of glass cases and came at last to a door marked 'Curator'. Mum knocked on the door.

'Come in!'

Mum opened the door and they went in. The room was light and airy but Claire had never seen so much clutter! There were books and files on every surface, and on the desk a framed family photograph was in danger of being tipped off the edge by an advancing heap of papers.

Mr Harris stood up and shook their hands. He smiled at them and immediately Claire felt at ease.

'Do sit down,' he said, seeing Mum's expanding waistline and at the same time looking despairingly at the only chair in the room which was already covered in files.

Mum smiled. 'Don't worry. We won't be a moment. We've only come to find out if the museum has anything about Stephanie House. We've just moved into the house and we wondered if you had any records – any information about the people who used to live there.'

Mr Harris remained standing. He rubbed his chin and thought for a while.

'Yes. Yes, I think I could dig out something for you. It's got quite an interesting history, I believe.'

As he chatted to Mum, Claire's eyes strayed to the family photo on his desk. There was a smiling woman with two children, a boy and a girl. Claire hoped she'd soon meet up with some children of her own age. Even though some of her old friends were coming to stay soon she'd like to get to know some of the local children before she started school here. She glanced up and saw that Mr Harris was looking at her. She blushed and he seemed to read her thoughts.

'I expect it's a bit strange, coming here from a big town,' he said.

Claire nodded but said nothing.

Mr Harris glanced at his watch. 'Look, I'm sorry but I'm afraid I'll have to go now. I've got to go to a meeting. I'll see what I can dig out about Stephanie House during the next few days.'

'That's very kind of you,' said Mum. 'Are you sure you have time?'

Mr Harris smiled. 'I shall enjoy it.' He collected some papers together and ushered them out. At the door he hesitated. 'If you like you could come to my house one evening and I could tell you what I've discovered.' He looked at Claire. 'You could meet my family, too. My daughter Laura is about your age.'

'I'd like that,' said Claire shyly.

'I'll be in touch soon, then,' promised Mr Harris as he hurried away.

After that they spent some time looking round the museum. Although it was small, there was plenty to see and Claire became quite absorbed. At last, the man at the kiosk came to tell them that the museum closed over the lunch-hour so they'd have to leave.

Mum looked at her watch. 'I had no idea it was so late,' she said.

As they headed for the front door, another visitor emerged from the museum and was ushered out. As Mum and Claire walked out into the sunlit courtyard, the other visitor hurried off. There was something about him that was vaguely familiar and Claire felt an inexplicable pang of fear. She watched the retreating back, clad in an expensive suit and city shoes and suddenly she recognised him. He was the man she'd seen looking at the house yesterday while she was unpacking books, the man the dog had barked at so ferociously. She gripped Mum by the arm. 'Look!' she said, pointing towards him. 'That's the man the dog barked at yesterday.'

Mum looked. 'Where? I can't see anyone.'

'There! Just turning the corner.'

Mum shrugged. 'No, sorry. I must have been looking in the wrong direction.'

When they got back to the house, Alec Toombs and his wife were just turning away from the front door. Mum heaved herself out of the car to greet them. 'I'm glad we didn't miss you,' she said.

Alec didn't care much for social chit-chat and he

came straight to the point. 'We've had a look round the garden. It's in a fair old state.'

His wife, Lizzie, chipped in. 'There's been no one in this place for three years. Its all gone to pieces.'

Mum looked around her and raised her eyebrows. 'I know. There's so much to be done.'

Lizzie Toombs gave her a knowing look and seeing the lines of fatigue round her eyes and her pale face, she touched her arm. 'Come on in then,' she said. 'You sit yourself down and tell me what's to be done in the house and Alec can make a start on the garden.'

Mum smiled and followed Lizzie into the house. Over her shoulder she said, 'Claire, go and show Alec where we've put all the garden things.'

Alec followed Claire round the back of the house to the garden shed and the dog followed them both, stopping often to sniff at the jungle that had once been a garden, or cock his leg against a tree.

Claire found all the things that Alex needed then she went inside. It was a hot day, so a little later, Mum sent her out with a drink for him. She found he'd already made an impression on the tangle of weeds and undergrowth and she stood for a moment watching him work with the steady rhythm of a born gardener. He stopped when he saw her, carefully wiped his brow and hands, propped up his long scythe by a tree then took his drink and sat down in the shade. All his movements were slow and deliberate. He was a man who made no unnecessary gestures and said no unnecessary words. In silence, he drank his drink, wiped his mouth, leant back and closed his eyes. Claire stood awkwardly beside him. She didn't want to disturb him, but something had been worrying her and she thought he might know the answer.

'Mr Toombs?'

Alec opened one eye and looked at her but he said nothing.

'Mr Toombs. Why's this house been empty for so long?'

The other eye opened and for a second he looked her full in the face. Then he looked down at his hands and his expression was completely blank. 'I couldn't say,' he said, then he handed back the empty mug, heaved himself to his feet and got on with his work.

'There *is* something strange about this house,' thought Claire as she walked slowly back with Alec's empty mug. 'People round here know something about it and they won't tell us what it is.'

The dog was at her heels, jumping up and whining as she moved off. She smiled and bent down to stroke his head. 'Shall we go for a walk, boy?'

At the word 'walk', the dog did some frenzied jumps and almost knocked Claire over. She laughed. 'OK, OK, hang on, fellow. I'll just tell them where we're going.'

In a few moments they were off, through the gate at the back of the house and into the field which ran steeply down to the river in the distance. The dog streaked ahead of Claire barking at butterflies, bouncing on imaginary enemies and occasionally coming back to lie panting on the ground and catch his breath for the next round. Claire walked slowly, enjoying the feel of grass beneath her feet and the warm summer smells. There was a lark overhead and Claire stared up at it as it hovered, calling with its shrill note. She was a city girl and she didn't know the bird was a lark, but she watched, fascinated, as it spiralled upwards again and then suddenly plummeted towards the ground. The river was still a thin sparkling band in the distance, but as she got nearer she could make out a tree-stump where the river bent sharply before continuing on its journey. Claire stopped with a sudden shock of recognition. She'd seen the tree-stump and the bend in the river before. Seen them clearly and unmistakably in the dream she'd had about the boy.

She walked on thoughtfully, chewing a piece of grass. The sun was warm on her back and there seemed to be no one else in the world but her and the dog. At last they reached the river and Claire made for the tree-stump and sat down. She looked down at the river and was surprised to see it was very deep. She'd been hoping to cup her hands and take a drink of water, but the sides were steep and muddy. The dog, however, knew exactly what to do. With one bound he was in the water and swimming happily, yapping at Claire who peered down at him from the river's edge. When he'd had enough, he scrambled up the steep bank and shook himself thoroughly, the water spraying Claire from head to toe. Then he flung himself down on the ground and stretched out in the sun. Claire smiled and sat down beside him, her back resting against the tree-stump. She was tired from the long walk and the sun was hot. She closed her eyes and listened to the birdsong and the hum of insects as the river slipped quietly by beneath her.

She didn't know whether she was asleep or awake, but suddenly he was there. The boy from last night's dream was there again! Claire rubbed her eyes and struggled to her feet and the dog was beside her, whining, its head on one side and its ears pricked. The boy was just as she had seen him in her dream but now he was standing on top of the tree-stump. He held something tightly in one hand but the other hand was pointing back towards the house and his face was full of anguish. Claire followed the pointing finger and,

36

although she could see nothing different, she suddenly felt, very strongly, as though she must get back. It was as though the house was calling to her, telling her she was needed there. She ran across the field, stumbling in her hurry, then staggered up the steep hill and it was only when she realised that the dog was not with her that she glanced back. The dog was beside the motionless figure of the boy and from where she stood they looked like one form. Then the boy stretched out his other hand towards Claire and this time the sun caught what he held and Claire saw – or thought she saw – a necklace of precious stones which threw a myriad of sparkling colours into the empty air.

Claire pressed on, her thoughts in frightening confusion. She dared not look up; she mustn't stop. She must get back to the house as quickly as possible. But the pain in her side forced her to stop at one point and she stood still, gasping for breath. As she looked down at the river again, the boy had disappeared and she could only see the dog. She shouted for him to follow her, but he remained where he was. At last she reached the fence which led into the garden, and only then did she look at the house.

It was exactly as she had left it! Claire stood at the fence, bewildered. Why had she felt so strongly that she needed to get back, that it was in some sort of danger? Alec was still scything the nettles and brambles in the garden and he nodded to her. Nothing had happened!

Claire turned back again to look at the river but there was nothing there and the only movement came from the dog who was streaking up the hill towards her.

## Chapter Four

Claire told no one what had happened by the river. She couldn't be sure whether she had really seen the boy or whether she had dreamt it again. But whether it was real or imagined, it stayed with her and she kept seeing the worry on the boy's face, his outstretched hand holding the sparkling necklace, and the dog, standing adoringly by his side.

But she refused to let it prey on her mind and, in any case, she had other things to think about. Two of her school friends were coming to visit and she pushed aside all other thoughts and determinedly ignored the insistent recurring dream of the boy by the tree-stump.

Time slipped by very happily. Claire enjoyed showing her old friends the house and the garden and together they explored the town and took the dog for walks in the surrounding countryside. But Claire kept away from the river.

It was nearly a month since they'd moved in, and the last of the visitors had just left when, one morning, the phone rang. It was Mr Harris, the curator of the museum, inviting Claire and her parents to his home the following Friday evening to meet his family and to look at the stuff he'd dug out about Stephanie House.

Dad came home earlier than usual that Friday. Claire was feeding the dog when he walked into the kitchen and she looked up and smiled. Dad hugged her briefly and put his hand down to stroke the dog. Then he said,

'Is Mum upstairs?' and when Claire nodded, he turned on his heel and went out of the room.

Although he said nothing, Claire sensed that something was not quite right. He nearly always cracked a joke or teased her when he came home but today he was much more serious than usual. Hardly knowing why she did it, Claire crept upstairs after him. Mum was resting on her bed and now Dad was in the bedroom too, pacing up and down, up and down, talking to her in a low voice.

Claire flattened herself against the wall outside and strained her ears to catch what they said.

'. . . finally got it out of them. Someone's been spreading the rumour that I'm not going to try and get the factory going again and that I'm only here to close it down. That I've got plans to build holiday houses on the site.'

'But that's ridiculous!' Claire could hear Mum heave herself off the bed and stand up.

'I know it's ridiculous.' Dad was almost shouting. 'But the rumour has really taken hold. Now everyone I approach is suspicious. The bank, the local newspaper, suppliers. If I don't get co-operation, we'll be ruined . . .'

There was more talk that Claire couldn't hear, then, 'But where did the rumours start – and who started them?'

Dad stopped pacing for a moment and Claire could hear him sigh. 'Who knows? No one seems to remember exactly who told them, but it's been well put about – people heard in the pub, in the supermarket, at the clinic. Someone's definitely trying to stop me. If I knew who was doing it, I could confront them but, as it is, I'm boxing at shadows.'

'Then you must talk to everyone at the factory. Tell

them the truth. You must squash the rumour at once before it takes hold.'

Claire heard Dad lower himself onto the bed. She pictured him with his head in his hands, frowning and bewildered at this completely unexpected turn of events. She crept along the passage to her room and stood at the window looking across the field to the river below. Then, trying to put what she'd heard out of her mind, she started to get ready to go out and visit the Harris family.

'Claire! Claire, are you ready?' Mum shouted from her room. Claire gave her hair a quick brush. 'Nearly,' she yelled back.

Then Dad's voice. 'I'll come with you, but Mum's going to stay here. She's a bit tired.'

Claire went into their room and kissed Mum goodbye.

'Mind you find out as much as you can about the house,' said Mum. 'And if you like the children, be sure to ask them round here.'

Claire nodded. 'Will you be all right?' she asked, suddenly anxious.

Mum smiled. 'Of course I'll be all right. I'm a bit tired, that's all.

Mr Harris lived with his family well outside the town, up a bumpy track which led them to a long low house which had once been three farm cottages. There were barns and a stable beside the house and it backed onto fields.

The garden was a tumbled blaze of colour and there were bikes thrown down on the lawn. The noise of family laughter drifted towards them through the open kitchen window.

The front door opened even before they got there and Mr Harris came down the path to meet them.

He led them through the house and into the kitchen to meet his wife and children. The children were called Laura and Tim. Laura was about Claire's age and Tim quite a lot younger. At first they were shy with each other but then Claire caught sight of a pony in the field at the back and asked if it belonged to Laura. Immediately, the ice was broken and moments later, Laura had fetched a headcollar and Claire was on the pony's back and being led round the field.

She loved the feel of the warm silky coat beneath her, but she couldn't stop sliding about.

'Grip with your knees and hang onto his mane,' said Laura, but Claire still slipped and soon they were both laughing.

'Look, I'll show you.' Laura helped Claire down from the pony's back then leapt on herself and, with only a halter, cantered bare back round the field, even taking in a few low jumps on the way.

'Show off,' shouted Tim, who had come out to join them. Laura ignored him and slithered to a halt beside Claire. Her face was pink and her eyes were shining.

'That was brilliant,' said Claire.

Laura got off the pony's back and flung her arms round his neck.

'I could teach you to ride if you like,' she said, but before Claire could answer, Mrs Harris shouted out to them, 'Not now, Laura. Claire and her dad have come to see something from the museum.' She paused. 'Perhaps Claire would like to come another time and spend the whole day here.'

Claire smiled and nodded. She'd almost forgotten why they'd come and now she was reluctant to go and look through lots of old papers. She gave the pony a pat then turned and went back inside the house.

In the sitting-room, Mr Harris had spread papers all over the floor. He and Dad were kneeling down looking at them and Claire went and squatted beside them.

'I haven't got any deeds,' said Mr Harris, 'but I should think that the original house was built in the late 16th century.'

'That's what we've been told,' said Dad.

'There's very little here about the early history of the house. It was altered and extended at various times, but for generations it belonged to the same family who farmed the land in much the same way for years. It was only later, in Victorian times, that things changed.'

'What happened then?' asked Claire. She stifled a yawn and her eyes slid to the window. Laura walked past, leading the pony, and waved.

With great care, Mr Harris picked up two or three very old newspapers. They were quite different from modern newspapers, thin and crackly and stained with age. He turned the pages until he found what he was looking for.

'In 1870, the eldest son of the farming family married a French girl called Stephanie Metier.'

Claire suddenly took an interest. 'Stephanie House! So the house was called after her then?'

Mr Harris nodded. 'That's right. She was apparently very beautiful and made a real stir in these parts. She was a city girl, used to all the glitter of Paris, and life in a farmhouse in the country must have seemed very dull.'

'I wonder how they met?' said Dad. 'I don't suppose farming folk travelled abroad much in those days.'

Mr Harris shrugged. 'Who knows. By all accounts, the family were very prosperous then. He may have been sent on a tour of Europe and have met her then. He seems to have been a very dashing young man. Their wedding was even reported in a national newspaper.' He jabbed his finger at the ageing newsprint and Claire and Dad leant forward to read the description of the wedding. 'Jocelyn Finbow and Stephanie Metier,' repeated Claire. 'It sounds very romantic.'

Mr Harris smiled. 'I think it probably was! From what I can gather, they were charming and popular. They entertained a lot and made frequent trips to Europe.'

'He can't have had much time for farming,' put in Dad.

'Ah,' said Mr Harris. 'You've hit the nail on the head, there! It appears that he was so besotted with his new wife and his social life that he neglected the land. Not long after his marriage, he was forced to sell land to pay for some of their extravagances. And this went on, year after year, and the estate got smaller and smaller.'

Claire stood up and stretched. 'Did they have any children?' she asked.

Mr Harris nodded. 'They had a son. I can't remember his name.' Mr Harris shuffled through some more papers. 'It's here somewhere . . .'

'Francis Pierre!' The name came unbidden to Claire's lips and without realising it, she had said it out loud.

Mr Harris looked up. 'Yes. Yes, that's right. I've found it now. How did you know?'

Dad was looking at her, too. No one spoke and the background of summery noises from the garden and the kitchen were suddenly unbearably loud.

Claire stood very still. How had she known? No one had told her. For what seemed an eternity, she couldn't answer, her tongue frozen and her mind shocked and confused. At last she shook her head to clear her thoughts and stuttered: 'I don't know. I suppose someone must have told me. Perhaps Mum . . .'

Dad continued to look puzzled, but Mr Harris went on. 'Yes, by all accounts, the boy was the apple of their eye. They both adored him. After he died, things were never the same again.'

Claire's heart started to beat faster and her hands became clammy with sweat. Long before the words were out of his mouth, she knew exactly what Mr Harris was going to say next. The intensity of the recurring dream she'd so resolutely pushed to the back of her mind, was with her once again and, without being told, she sensed that the boy had died young, sensed how he had died and even where he had died. Yet no one had told her. She was shaken by this sudden foreknowledge, and her face was very pale as she listened to the story unfold.

Mr Harris put the old newspapers down and smoothed them flat. 'It was a tragic story. The boy fell into the river.'

'He drowned, then?' asked Dad.

'Well, no, he didn't. He very nearly drowned, but he was rescued by his dog. The dog apparently jumped into the river and dragged the boy to safety, then the boy managed to scramble back up the bank and get home.'

'So how did he die?'

'He died of pneumonia, about three weeks later.'

They were all silent with their own thoughts. Claire, in her mind's eye, could see Francis' small fevered body tossing and turning on his bed, fighting for his life, while his anxious parents watched over him. And then, finally, giving up the battle as his spirit drifted from its earthly shell.

And all this had happened, she knew, without a shadow of doubt, in what was now her own bedroom at Stephanie House.

Claire was so absorbed in her own thoughts that she only heard snatches of the rest of the story of Jocelyn and Stephanie, of how Stephanie became pregnant again and then died giving birth to a stillborn child and how Jocelyn retired from the world and became a distraught old man, finally leaving nothing but debts and a decaying house when he died.

'What a sad story,' said Dad.

'It began with such glitter and romance and ended in bitterness and ruin,' said Mr Harris. 'After that, the house was sold and passed through various hands, as you know.'

Dad got up from the floor. 'You've done a lot of research to find out about the house for us,' he said.

Mr Harris stood up too, and stretched. 'I've found it very interesting.' Then he went on. 'Funnily enough, someone else has been asking about its history, so I'll be well prepared when he comes to the museum tomorrow.'

Claire looked up sharply. The strange man again. It must be! Why did he want to know about Stephanie House? Why was he so interested?

She was about to ask who the man was, but Mr Harris had remembered something else. 'Oh, I brought this along for you to see. It came to the museum some years ago.' He picked up a small oval painting set in a delicate frame of pearls and gold and handed it to Dad. 'That's a portrait of Stephanie Finbow.'

Dad looked at it. 'She's beautiful,' he said. 'No wonder poor Jocelyn went mad when she died.'

Claire stood on tiptoe to look.

It was an exquisite miniature portrait of a dark-haired young woman in a low-cut dress. But Claire hardly glanced at her face for something else immediately caught her attention. Round the slender neck hung a beautiful necklace of precious jewels. Claire knew nothing of jewellery, but words, again, came unbidden to her mind. 'Enamelled gold, set with rose and brilliant-cut diamonds, rubies, emeralds, pearls and a sapphire.'

It was a necklace she had seen before – in the outstretched hand of the boy in her dreams.

Suddenly, Claire couldn't bear to be in the room any longer. She excused herself and went in search of Laura and Tim. She found them with Mrs Harris, in the kitchen, and soon she was sitting at the kitchen table, drinking homemade lemonade and chatting to Laura about the pony, about the school, about everything, in fact, except Stephanie House.

As they were leaving, Laura said. 'Can Claire come over tomorrow. I could show her where we swim and everything.'

Mrs Harris smiled. 'Of course. If she'd like to.'

Claire accepted and Mrs Harris turned to say good-bye to Dad.

Then Claire remembered what Mum had said. 'You and Tim could come to Stephanie House if you like,' she said.

'No way,' said Tim fiercely, 'I'm not going near that nouse.'

Laura rounded on him. 'Shut up, Tim.'

Tim shrugged and mooched off to find his bike.

Claire frowned and looked at Laura for an explanation. 'What's the matter with Tim,' she said.

'Oh don't take any notice,' said Laura. She took Claire firmly by the arm. 'Come and see the guinea-pigs before you go.'

# Chapter Five

It was a long time before Claire got to sleep that night. She tried to make herself think of Laura and the pony and of all the things that Laura had said they could do the next day. But it was no good. Pleasant thoughts were crowded out and the sad story of Stephanie House took over. The pleading face of young Francis Finbow swam into focus every time she closed her eyes and Tim's parting words nagged at her, giving substance to the fear she had had at the back of her mind ever since she arrived here. The fear that something bad might happen to them in this house, for despite its beauty and warmth, she realised now that its tragic history had left a mark. Claire could feel the sadness; it seeped into the atmosphere, sighed on the summer breeze and echoed in the cries of the owl that swept over the fields and down towards the river. And nowhere was the feeling stronger than here, in her bedroom. The room in which young Francis had died.

She couldn't get Tim's parting words out of her mind. 'I'm not going near *that* house.' Why had he said that? People round here must know something about Stephanie House; there was something strange about it that no one would explain. Alec Toombs hadn't replied when she'd asked him why the house had been empty for so long and the man at the museum office had suddenly paid attention when they'd mentioned Stephanie House. Local people were all suspicious of the house – but *why*?

When she did finally drift off to sleep, it was only to dream vividly. Again she saw Francis, standing by the river, his face drawn with anxiety and his arms outstretched towards her. And again he held the priceless necklace in his hand. In her dream, Claire pleaded with him. 'What *is* it? What's the matter? What do you want me to do?' She muttered these questions in her sleep and tossed and turned in bed but there was no reply and no change of expression from the boy in her dream.

But there was some noise, some very real noise in the bedroom. It came from beside her and eventually it penetrated her unconscious and dragged her awake. She turned over to look at her clock and met the dog's wet nose that was pushing into her body for attention. The dog was trembling at her side, whining in the darkness in just the same way that he'd whined before, when she'd seen Francis near the tree-stump beside the river. Claire put out her hand to stroke the dog's silky head and this seemed to calm him. After a moment, the trembling and the whining stopped and he started to lick Claire's hand.

'It's all right, boy. I expect I was talking in my sleep. It was just a dream,' said Claire. But she said it without much conviction.

Claire glanced at the clock. It was only three am. She sighed and tried to settle down again, but the dog wouldn't leave her alone and kept butting his head into her neck. Eventually, Claire sat up and, thinking the dog needed to go out, she swung her legs over the bed and felt with her toes for her slippers. She bent to put them on, feeling in the darkness, and when she looked up again the dog was suddenly quite still by her side. Still and alert. Slowly, Claire turned her head towards the window. For some reason she couldn't explain, she knew what she was going to see and, perhaps because she knew, she wasn't afraid.

There by the window, was the figure she had glimpsed once before, on that first night, but this time the image didn't fade immediately. Small and elegant, with dark flowing hair, the woman stood with one hand resting on her swollen stomach and the other fingering the precious stones which encircled her neck.

'Enamelled gold, set with rose and brilliant-cut diamonds, rubies, emeralds, pearls and a sapphire.'

Claire had no idea how long she stared at the figure and she had no idea how she knew so much about the necklace, but again the unfamiliar words had formed themselves in her mind and she knew they were right. The woman hardly moved, but the light breeze from the open window ruffled her hair and the jewels of the necklace softly reflected the pale moonlight.

Then, suddenly, the dog sprang away from Claire's caressing hand and started to scratch at the rug in the middle of the floor, whining as he did so. As his frantic scrabbling increased in tempo, so the outline of the woman gradually disappeared until there was nothing to see except the large window and the new curtains, hung that day. They were drawn apart a little to let in the air and they moved rhythmically in the breeze just as the woman's hair had moved.

For a long time, Claire continued to sit and stare towards the window. Then, at last, she shivered slightly, broke out of her trance and switched on the bedside light. The dog seemed to relax, too. He stopped digging at the floor, had a shake and a scratch, then jumped onto the end of the bed and settled down.

'It's just my imagination,' said Claire, out loud to the dog. But she knew it wasn't and suddenly she felt as though it was all too much for her. The dog went to sleep almost immediately but Claire stayed wide awake and she sat rigidly upright, hugging her knees. She could no longer pretend that the atmosphere in the house wasn't affecting her and she could no longer push to the back of her mind her fear that, for some reason she couldn't possibly understand, her family was in danger.

'Tomorrow I'll tell Mum,' she thought. 'I'll tell her properly, all about the dreams and the room and Francis and everything . . .'

She felt better then, and at last she snuggled under the duvet and fell into a deep sleep.

But she didn't sleep for long. The clock in the hall had just struck four when the sound of voices from her parents' room woke her up again. She heard her father talking on the telephone and the snap of the light switch in the passage.

Claire switched on her light again and got out of bed. She had just reached her door when her father came in. He was fully dressed and his face was pale. He took Claire's hand, led her back to her bed and sat down.

'What's the matter? Why are you up so early? What's happened?' Claire's voice was shrill.

Her father didn't hide his anxiety and he said, without preamble, 'It's Mum. We'll have to get her to the hospital. She's a bit worried about the baby.'

Claire stared at her father in disbelief. They had all waited so long for this baby. Mum had almost resigned herself to having no more children when at last she'd become pregnant. Surely it couldn't all go wrong now?

Dad squeezed her shoulder. 'Get dressed quickly, love. We're leaving right away.'

Claire whispered, 'Yes,' and turned her face away. As her father walked out of the door and she struggled into her clothes, she said fiercely into the room, 'Please don't do this to us. Please let the baby live. Please let Mum be all right.' She finished dressing and, just before she left, she closed her eyes and pressed her hands to her head, trying to imagine the small anxious figure of Francis, but too many thoughts were crowding in and she couldn't. Instead, she murmured again, 'Please! I'll try and do what you want me to do. I promise I'll try. Only please don't harm us.'

Claire remembered very little of the drive to the hospital and the long wait there. As soon as they arrived, Mum was put in a wheelchair and hurried away with Dad at her side. Someone gave Claire a cup of tea and once or twice, nurses came to talk to her, but she was hardly aware of the hurrying feet, the clanging of trollies and the constant ringing of the telephone, for all the time she was pleading in her mind with the troubled spirits of Stephanie House. 'Please let the baby live. Please let Mum be all right. Let me know what you want me to do and I'll try and do it. Please, please don't let anything bad happen to us.'

She must have drifted off to sleep once because she saw Francis again, and although in her dream she still had no guidance from him, when she awoke, lolling awkwardly on the hospital chair, she knew, instinctively, that in some way it was the necklace which was the reason for the atmosphere at Stephanie House and the unease of its long departed occupants.

Claire sat upright and stretched. She was stiff and very tired, but she felt much calmer. If she could find out more about the necklace, then she might be able to help them all – Mum and the baby as well as Dad and the people at the factory. For she was quite certain now, that in some way she couldn't possibly understand, it was all connected.

'What did you say, dear?' The nurse at the desk looked up and Claire blushed, realising she'd been muttering out loud.

'Er . . . nothing. I just wondered what was happening to Mum.'

'I'll see if I can find out for you,' said the nurse, and, turning her back on Claire, she dialled a number on the telephone and murmured confidentially into the mouthpiece. Then she replaced the receiver and faced Claire. Her expression betrayed absolutely nothing.

'Your Dad's coming down to fetch you.'

Claire looked up sharply.

At last she saw Dad, walking slowly towards her. She went to meet him and he put his arm round her.

'Is Mum all right?'

'Yes. Mum's fine now. You can go and see her in a minute.'

'What about the baby?'

Dad said nothing for a moment, then he cleared his throat but, even so, his voice was hoarse. 'Mum's just got to be very careful for the next few weeks. The doctors want her to stay in hospital so she can get lots of rest and they can keep an eye on her.'

'But will the baby be all right?'

Dad gave her a squeeze. 'Yes, I'm sure the baby will be all right. But it's best that Mum stays here until it's born, just to make certain nothing goes wrong.'

Claire nodded slowly, absorbing all that this meant. 'Can I go and see Mum?'

Mum was pale and tired, but she held Claire close to her and hugged her.

'It won't be for long, darling. Just a week or two, until the baby's born. Dad's going to telephone Granny and ask her to come early to look after you both.'

Claire made a face at Dad. 'Why can't we manage

on our own? I'm twelve years old and Dad's not a bad cook!'

Mum laughed. 'Well, his cooking's better than his carpentry, I must admit!' Then she went on, 'But I don't want Dad worrying about where you are all day. I want someone in the house with you.'

'What about Lizzie Toombs, then?' said Claire. 'Perhaps she could come up to the house more often.'

Secretly, she thought that any arrangement would be better than having Granny fussing around her all day. Granny was OK in small doses, and if Mum had been there, with a new baby, Granny wouldn't have had much time to worry about Claire. But just the two of them in the house together all day would be awful. Meals would always have to be exactly on time, Claire would always have to say exactly where she was going. Desperately, she tried to think of an alternative.

'What about the Harrises,' said Claire brightly. 'I'm spending the day there tomorrow. I really like Laura and I'm sure they wouldn't mind having me for some of the time . . . perhaps when Lizzie couldn't come up to the house.'

Mum looked doubtful. 'Oh, I don't know, love. I haven't even met Mrs Harris.'

'They're a very nice family,' put in Dad, winking at Claire.

Mum was beginning to weaken. 'Whose side are you on?' she said, turning to Dad. But she was smiling.

Dad grinned sheepishly and didn't answer. Claire grabbed her chance.

'At least let's ask them – and Lizzie. Surely, between us we'll be able to manage?'

'All right, then. Ask them if you like. But if there's any problem, I want Granny to come. Understand? I don't want my family being a burden to anyone.'

53

They left Mum to rest and Claire skipped ahead of Dad to the elevator. When he caught her up, he was grinning from ear to ear. 'You little minx!' he said.

'What do you mean? I was doing you a favour. You know what Granny's like!'

Dad chuckled. 'Oh yes,' he said, 'I know what Granny's like!'

They walked, hand-in-hand out to the car-park.

## Chapter Six

Dad and Claire went to see Lizzie Toombs not long after they got back from the hospital, and even before they'd asked she'd offered to come up to the house every day, if necessary. She enfolded Claire in her comfortable arms and Dad backed away a little nervously, in case he got the same treatment.

It was late morning before they arrived at the Harris's house. Mrs Harris took one look at them and immediately ushered them into the kitchen and sat them down.

'What's happened?' she asked. 'You both look exhausted!'

So Dad explained, and Mrs Harris said immediately, 'Why don't you come and stay here, Claire, while your mum's in hospital? There's plenty of room.'

Claire was on the point of accepting, when she thought of Dad, alone in the evenings and of Stephanie House, empty and rejected. It would be so easy to stay here, in warmth and comfort away from the frightening dreams and feelings she'd experienced. Part of her longed to say yes, but another, tougher part, wanted to fight back; although she didn't know what it was, she was sure there was something she had to do at Stephanie House if she was to break this run of bad luck. Claire didn't want to seem rude but neither did she want to lose contact with Stephanie House, not now that she had just begun to have a glimmer of understanding. At last she said, 'I don't want to leave the animals.'

'You could bring the dog here,' said Mrs Harris at once.

'And Lizzie or I can feed the cat,' said Dad.

Claire looked down at her hands. 'If you don't mind, I think I'd rather sleep at home.' Although they'd been there several weeks, it was the first time she had called Stephanie House 'home', and all at once she felt that it *was* really her home and she wanted fiercely to hang onto it and be part of it.

Mrs Harris came and put an arm round Claire's shoulders. 'I think that's a very good idea,' she said. 'Then you can be with Dad when he comes back from work and you can visit your Mum together.'

She looked over Claire's head at Dad and he smiled his thanks, then he said to Claire, 'I'll come and fetch you this evening, after work and we can go to the hospital together.'

Laura, who had been hovering in the background suddenly broke in. 'Where's the dog now?'

Claire turned her head. 'We left him in the back garden. He'll be all right today but he gets lonely. I'll bring him tomorrow.'

'We could ride back and fetch him if you like,' said Laura.

Claire brightened. 'OK,' she said. 'That would be great.'

They waved goodbye to Dad, then Laura led Claire round to the paddock. Tim had gone to a friend for the morning, so they were alone, and Claire was secretly relieved.

For the next hour or so, Claire almost forgot all her worries. Laura taught her how to groom the pony, pick out his feet and tack him up. Gradually, Claire became more confident at handling all the unfamiliar gear. She loved the smell and the warmth of the pony, the gentle blowing from his nostrils and his nudges against her side as he looked hopefully for a carrot or pony-nut in the pocket of her jacket. She brushed him until he shone then stood back with pride to admire his gleaming coat.

'Now for your riding lesson,' said Laura. She helped Claire put on a hard hat and showed her how to mount.

At first Claire was tense and nervous, but gradually she began to relax and enjoy herself. It took the rest of the morning, but at last she learnt to trot without banging about in the saddle.

'You've got it!' said Laura, clapping her hands above her head and jumping up and down. Claire beamed with pleasure.

'Now canter.'

'What?'

'Kick him on and sit down in the saddle. He knows what to do.'

Claire did as Laura said and, to her surprise, the pony responded immediately. His pace quickened and soon they were doing a steady canter round the paddock.

'This is brilliant,' shouted Claire, as she thundered past Laura.

Claire did several more circuits at trot and then at canter until Laura was satisfied, then they unsaddled the pony and put him in the stable.

Claire's face was pink with effort when they went into the house for lunch and Mrs Harris congratulated her. 'I was watching from the window,' she said. 'You did really well.'

'It was great,' said Claire.

Mrs Harris started to serve out the lunch. 'You'll be stiff tomorrow. You've been using all sorts of muscles you don't normally use.

Claire rubbed her legs. 'I know. They already feel like jelly!'

The front door slammed and Tim came crashing into the kitchen, his face and hands streaked with mud, bursting to tell them about where he'd been and what he'd been doing. Mrs Harris cut into his chatter.

'OK, OK, we'll listen when we're eating. Go and wash your hands.'

'I'm starving!' he said, as he put a token splash of water onto his hands then rubbed the rest of the dirt onto the kitchen towel.

Claire was starving too. She and Dad had forgotten about breakfast and she was very empty. She attacked with enthusiasm a large helping of shepherd's pie and then made short work of some fruit salad and ice-cream.

They all helped Mrs Harris clear the table and put the dishes in the dishwasher.

'Can we ride over to Stephanie House and get the dog now?' asked Laura. 'Claire can go on my bike and I'll take the pony.'

Mrs Harris nodded. 'Yes, if you like. But make sure you're back by tea-time.' Then she turned to Tim. 'Do you want to go with them?'

Tim yawned and stretched his arms high above his head. 'No way,' he said again. 'I'm not going near that place.'

Mrs Harris frowned at him and Laura cut in quickly. 'Well if you stay here you can clean out the guinea-pigs.'

'No. Why should I?'

'Because I did them last week and it's your turn.'

'Oh shut up, they don't need cleaning out.'

Mrs Harris interrupted. 'Off you go girls. Tim and I will see to the guinea-pigs.'

58

'Oh Mum,' said Laura. 'It's not fair. I know what'll happen. You'll end up cleaning them out. Tim *never* does it.'

'Oh stop moaning,' said Tim. 'What does it matter who does it so long as they get done.'

'But I don't see why Mum should . . .'

'I won't,' said Mrs Harris firmly. 'Tim will, before I take him swimming.'

'Hey, are we going swimming!'

'Only if you do the guinea-pigs first.'

At this point, Laura and Claire slipped out of the kitchen. 'You're so lucky not to have a brother,' said Laura, then, realising at once what she'd said, put her hand on Claire's arm. 'Oh, I'm sorry. I forgot. You might have one soon – or a sister.

Claire stopped at the back door. Outside, the sun was shining and the garden was a mass of colour. Everywhere there was growth and energy and life. She turned to look at Laura and said, 'Do you think everything will be all right with Mum and the baby?'

'Of course it will,' said Laura. 'You'll see. In a couple of weeks there'll be a bouncing baby at Stephanie House and I'll come over and help you bath it! Come on, we'll get the bike and the pony and go over there now.'

But Claire hesitated. She had to tell someone about what was happening to her at Stephanie House and she couldn't worry Mum now. Every time she thought about it, she felt as though she would burst if she didn't share her feelings soon and, although she hardly knew Laura, she liked her a lot and thought she might understand. She took a deep breath and decided to risk it.

'Wait a minute, Laura. Before we go, I want to tell

you something. Something about the house.' She hesitated, not meeting Laura's eyes, and picked nervously at an imaginary piece of fluff on her jeans. 'I haven't told anyone else but I must talk to someone about it soon.' She looked around. 'Can we find somewhere to talk?'

Laura frowned. 'OK,' she said, sounding puzzled. 'I suppose so. We'll go and sit in the stable. Tim never goes in there,' she added.

They walked in silence over to the stable. Claire felt quite weak; her muscles were beginning to stiffen up and the lack of sleep had caught up with her. There were two stalls in a big stable beside the paddock and Claire sank thankfully onto a straw bale outside the stall where the pony stood, pushing his neck over the bar for a stroke or a carrot.

Laura came and sat down beside her and for a moment neither of them spoke. Claire plucked a straw from the bale and picked at it with her nail. Then she began.

Laura said nothing as Claire told her about the atmosphere in her bedroom at Stephanie House, about the dream child, Francis, whose image was so strong that she'd even seen him during the day by the river. About the dog and her certainty that it was, in some way, a link between past and present. And about the beautiful Stephanie Finbow and her necklace and the strange man who seemed so interested in the house.

Finally, she told her, haltingly, about the trouble at her Dad's work, about the rumours and suspicion and her feeling that if only she could uncover the truth about the necklace and about the strange man, this in some way would stop their run of bad luck.

When she'd finished speaking she felt drained. But

she felt relieved, too, that at last she'd been able to voice all her fears.

She looked at Laura. 'Do you believe me?'

Laura stood up and went over to the pony. She stroked his nose and patted him. Then she turned to face Claire, her arm hanging loosely over the pony's neck.

'Bad luck house,' she muttered.

'What?'

'That's what everyone round here calls it,' she said. 'Bad luck house. For years, the people living there have had bad luck.'

Claire looked up sharply. 'What sort of bad luck?'

Laura shrugged. 'All sorts of bad luck. Accidents, money troubles. Oh, I don't know but no one ever stays there and in the end no local person would buy it.'

'Why didn't anyone tell us!'

'Your family came from a long way away. No one knew you. Why should anyone tell you. Anyway, it's only local gossip.'

Claire shook her head. 'No, it's more than that. There really is something – a sort of curse – but I'm *sure* it can be broken. I *know* I'm being given some clues.'

She got up and went over to where Laura was standing. 'Do you think I'm crazy?'

Laura went on stroking the pony's nose and didn't look at Claire. 'No,' she said slowly. 'No, I don't think you're crazy. But it's just hard to take in, that's all. Specially when I haven't seen the boy or the woman or the necklace.'

'You think I'm making it up, don't you?' said Claire, her voice dull.

'No,' said Laura, looking her straight in the eye. 'I

do believe you, I promise. Anyway, why should you make it up?'

Claire looked about her. 'It seems so silly, talking about it here, where everything is so ordinary. But honestly, Laura, Stephanie House is quite different from any other house.' She frowned, trying to find words to describe the atmosphere that seeped into her whole being while she was there. In the end, she said, rather lamely, 'You get a sort of special feeling there.'

'OK,' said Laura. 'Let's go and get the dog. Then you can show me your room and everything and maybe I'll understand.'

They saddled up the pony again and Laura fetched her bike from the garage. Claire got on the bike and headed for the front gate.

'No – we'll go this way,' said Laura, pointing to the far side of the paddock. 'There's a good bridle path that goes all the way to Stephanie House. It's a bit bumpy for the bike but it's much shorter than going on the road.'

Laura rode up to a gate in the fence that led on to the fields beyond. Claire opened it and they went through, keeping to the path that went diagonally across the field, then dropped down to follow the river. The pony trotted easily along, but Claire found biking very hard work. After about ten minutes, Laura stopped the pony.

'Why don't you ride the pony now and I'll bike?'

They changed over, and from her elevated position, Claire could see the lie of the land.

'Oh I can see where we are now,' she said. 'I came here with the dog a few weeks ago.'

In a few more minutes, they rode past the tree-stump where Claire had seen the boy Francis. She looked carefully about her, but today there was no sign of anything unusual, just the willows moving slightly in the breeze and the river flowing between steep banks beneath them.

'Is this where you swim,' she asked.

'No way!' said Laura, between puffs. 'It's too dangerous.' She jerked a thumb behind her. 'There's a pool back there where the river widens out. It's really nice. I'll take you there one day.'

At last they came in sight of the hill that led up to the back of Stephanie House. Laura got off the bike.

'I'll have to push it up here,' she said. 'You go ahead and I'll catch you up.'

Nervously, Claire urged the pony on up the hill and soon they had left Laura several metres behind. As they approached the house, Claire saw two figures talking in the back garden. One was Alec Toombs, but it wasn't until she got closer that she recognised the other one. Her heart started racing and in some way her unease transmitted itself to the pony. He shied and stepped off the path and Claire was almost unseated. By the time she'd put her feet back in the stirrups, gathered up the reins again and given the pony a reassuring pat, the other man had gone.

It was the man she'd seen before. The man whom she'd seen staring at the house. The man in the museum. What was he doing here? And why was he talking to Alec?

All Claire's fear and uncertainty came flooding back. She didn't want to go on alone and she waited until Laura came up beside her.

'What's the matter? Why did you stop?'

Claire cleared her throat. 'You know the man I told you about, the man we saw in the museum. The one who was staring at the house?'

Laura nodded.

'Well, he was here, just now. Talking to Alec in the garden.'

Laura shielded her eyes with her hand and looked towards the house. All she saw was Alec, busy again with his digging. She gave Claire a strange look and said nothing.

'He *was* there, Laura. He *was*!'

'OK, OK. I believe you.' But she didn't sound convinced and they continued in silence until they reached the garden fence.

They went in through the back gate. Alec acknowledged their presence with a brief nod of the head but he didn't stop his slow, steady digging. They found an iron ring set into the wall of a tumbledown shed that had once been a stable and Laura slipped a headcollar over the pony's bridle and tied him securely to the ring. Then they walked round to the front of the house. As they passed Alec, Claire paused, but his expression left her in no doubt that he wanted to get on with his work, so she didn't speak to him.

The dog was at the front gate, barking and growling, apparently at nothing. Claire called him and he came rushing towards her, tail wagging, a whip-thin muscled tornado, all aggression forgotten. He leapt up at her, his dirty paws on her chest and his wet nose as near her face as possible.

'No, boy,' said Claire, as the dog tried to push past them into the house. 'I want to show Laura something. You can stay outside until I've finished.'

She let herself into the house and Laura followed, a few paces behind.

They stopped for a moment in the hall, bathed in the afternoon light that flooded through the big window on the landing.

'It's lovely,' whispered Laura. She'd never been into

Stephanie House before and she felt rather overawed, by its reputation, its atmosphere but, most of all, by its ageless beauty.

There was a smell of baking coming from the kitchen and they found Lizzie there, making enough pies to feed an army. She grinned at them broadly. 'Just a few things for your freezer,' she said, wiping her hands on her apron. Then she made them sit down and gave them jam tarts and a cool drink.

'Lizzie,' said Claire, between bites of crumbling pastry, 'You've known this house for ages. Have people always had bad luck here?'

Lizzie looked across at Laura. 'What have you been telling her?' she asked accusingly. Then she turned back to Claire. 'Don't you go believing any nonsense like that.'

'But it's true, isn't it?' persisted Claire.

Carefully, Lizzie lowered her comfortable bulk onto the chair next to Claire.

'I can't deny there's been some bad luck happen to people here,' she said at last, 'but that's no reason why bad luck should come your way.'

'It already has,' thought Claire to herself. Aloud, she said, 'I keep having these funny dreams, all about the family that used to live here years ago. The Finbows.'

She found it easy to talk to Lizzie. She was solid and warm and comforting.

'Ah yes, I've heard of them,' said Lizzie. 'It was a sad story.'

Then she heaved herself up. 'Well, I must get on with my cooking.' She picked up a rolling pin and pointed it at Claire. 'Now, if you've got any worries while your mum's away, you come straight to me and tell me about them.'

Claire smiled. 'OK, I will.'

'You promise?'

'Promise,' said Claire. She scraped back her chair and stood up. 'I'm just going to show Laura the rest of the house.'

Claire led the way upstairs to her bedroom. As always, when she walked in through the door, she sensed the change in temperature. Laura followed her. She stood looking out of the window for a moment then, without thinking, started to rub her arms.

'It's cold . . .' she began, then stopped and stared at Claire.

Claire said nothing. She propelled Laura out of the door and into her parents' room. The temperature in the passage and in her parents' room was different; it was much warmer.

They went back again to Claire's room.

'Wait here,' said Claire, 'I want to show you something.' And she went downstairs and returned with an irritable and sleepy Dodo. With the cat in her arms, she walked into her bedroom and gently shut the door with her back.

The cat's reaction was immediate. He leapt from Claire's arms, his fur raised in terror, and scrabbled desperately at the closed door, yowling to be let out.

Claire opened the door for him and he shot out, a startled ginger bottle-brush. Then she turned back and looked at Laura.

Laura nodded, and when she spoke, her voice was serious. 'Yes. Yes I did feel it. I do feel it. I think there *is* something here that we can't understand.'

Claire sighed deeply. 'Then you believe me? You don't think I'm crazy?'

'Yes,' she said slowly, 'I really do believe you now.'

*

They collected the dog and retraced their steps. Claire went to talk to Alec, feeling less uncertain now that she knew Laura believed her. Reluctantly, he stopped digging.

'Mr Toombs, who were you talking to just before we arrived?'

Alec showed no surprise. 'Some fellow who was interested in the house. Said his family used to live near here years ago.'

'What's his name?'

'Blest if I can remember,' said Alec, scratching the back of his hand. Then he rummaged in his trouser pocket.

'He gave me this,' he said, showing a crumpled business card to Claire. 'Said if your dad ever wanted to sell the house, he'd be interested in buying it.'

'But we've only just arrived!'

'That's what I told him,' said Alec, 'But he kept on at me. Said to be sure to give his message to your dad.'

'I'll give it to him,' said Claire. She looked at the writing on the card. 'Jeremy Knight,' she read. Then she saw the words underneath.

Still frowning at the card, she said goodbye to Alec, then she and Laura, with the pony and the dog, went out into the field and onto the bridlepath.

'Well,' said Laura at last. 'Aren't you going to tell me? What's his name? Who is he?'

Claire was walking beside the pony, pushing the bike. She looked up. 'His name is Jeremy Knight,' she said, 'And he's a jeweller.'

## Chapter Seven

As soon as they were down the hill and beside the river, out of Alec's sight, they stopped.

'Do you think this Knight man really wants to buy the house,' asked Laura, sliding off the pony's back and slipping the reins over his head.

Claire propped the bike against a tree and looked down at the water which flowed with deceptive sluggishness beneath her. It had the appearance of calm, but she knew from what Laura had told her that there was a strong current beneath. Like Stephanie House, she thought. Calm and peaceful on the outside, but full of secrets inside. Out loud, she said, 'I don't know. I shouldn't think so. But I do know he wants to get inside it.'

'But why? What for?' asked Laura.

Claire didn't answer at once. Now that she knew the name of the mysterious man and what he did, an idea was slowly forming in her mind. She thought she knew, now, why Jeremy Knight was so interested in the house and, if she was right, then all her dreams made some sort of sense.

She came over to the pony and stroked his nose. At last, she said, slowly, 'I think Jeremy Knight wants to get into the house because something is hidden there – something he wants very badly.'

Laura looked puzzled. 'What? What could he possibly want?'

Claire went on, thoughts clarifying in her mind as

she spoke. 'I'm sure that somehow he's found out about the necklace, the one in the portrait, the one that I keep dreaming about. I think it's probably very valuable.'

Laura's eyes widened as she realised what Claire meant. 'And you think it's still at Stephanie House?'

Claire nodded. 'I'm certain it's hidden somewhere in the house and I think Jeremy Knight knows it too.'

'But how could he possibly know?'

Claire shrugged. 'I haven't a clue. But I'm certain he's found out about it.'

Laura whistled. 'If you're right, shouldn't we tell someone?'

Claire frowned. 'If there was anything to tell, I would. But what could I say to Dad – or to anyone else? At the moment, it's all in my mind.'

They were silent for a moment, then Claire went on. 'There's something else, too.'

'What?'

'I think that Stephanie Finbow died before she could tell anyone about the necklace. I think she kept it a secret from everyone – even her husband. The necklace must have meant something very special to her and now that Jeremy Knight has found out about it, she wants *us* to keep it out of his hands.'

Laura stared at her. 'But how do you know all this?'

Claire frowned. How could she explain something she didn't understand herself? 'I don't *know*,' she said quietly. 'I can't explain it, Laura. But I feel it. I feel sure I'm right. Stephanie's restless spirit has somehow affected everyone who has come to live in the house. If only we can give her peace, we shall be able to live here in peace ourselves.'

'But why should *you* know all this? Why haven't the

other people known. People who were in the house before you?'

Claire shrugged. 'I don't know, unless . . . unless the necklace has never been in danger before. Perhaps that's it. Perhaps that's why the presence of Stephanie and Francis is so strong at the moment.'

Laura looked away. She found it very hard to accept all this talk of spirits. She fiddled with the pony's reins.

Suddenly, the dog stiffened beside them. He started to whine, and ignoring Claire's calls, he ran flat out, straight along the path beside the river and back towards Laura's house.

The girls mounted the pony and the bike and followed him.

'What's he doing?' said Laura, as she watched him slither to a halt and sit quietly, panting with effort and apparently looking up at nothing.

Claire shivered, but not from cold. She sensed what was going to happen because the dog was at the tree-stump where she'd seen Francis. She got off the bike and put her hand across the pony's neck and over Laura's arm.

'Shh. Keep still,' she whispered. 'Look!'

Laura kept her eyes on the dog. He sat motionless now and both girls watched as, out of nowhere, the figure of a slightly-built boy took form, standing on top of the tree-stump. As the image became clearer, they saw something in the boy's outstretched hand, something that sparkled in the sunlight filtering through the willow trees.

Then Laura blinked – and the figure had disappeared.

'Did you see him Laura?' said Claire. And again, more urgently. 'Did you see him?'

Laura swallowed nervously and looked at Claire. 'Yes,' she said quietly. 'Yes I did see him.'

They made their way slowly back beside the river, unnerved by the experience and shy of speaking about it to each other. At last Claire cleared her throat and broke the awkward silence. 'We've got to find out about that necklace,' she said, as she stood up on the bike and negotiated the bumpy track.

'And about Jeremy Knight,' added Laura.

They came in sight of Laura's house and the pony started to dance with excitement.

'I'll give him a gallop here,' said Laura. She felt she needed to break away from what she'd seen by the tree-stump. She'd been shocked and frightened by the figure of Francis Finbow. Up until that moment, she hadn't really known what to make of Claire's story. She liked Claire very much but she didn't know her well, didn't know whether all her talk about spirits and jewels should be taken seriously.

But now it was different. She'd seen Francis Finbow with her own eyes and she had no doubts at all. She believed everything Claire had told her and she felt, like her, that it was up to them to try and save the necklace.

With gentle pressure from her legs she urged the pony on and soon they were galloping over the grass towards home. Claire pedalled behind and watched as the pounding hooves and flying tail disappeared round the next bend in the river. She felt envious of Laura's easy skill and the way in which the horse and rider complemented one another.

Laura was unsaddling the pony by the time Claire got back and Mr Harris was beside them, patting the pony and talking to Laura.

As soon as she saw Laura's father, Claire remembered something. Jeremy Knight had been to see Mr Harris at the museum to find out about Stephanie House. Mr Harris might know something more about this mysterious jeweller.

She propped the bike up beside the stable and went over to him.

'Hello, Claire,' he said. 'I hear you're turning into quite a jockey.'

Claire smiled shyly. 'Laura's a really good teacher,' she said, then she dug into the pocket of her jacket and brought out the mud-stained crumpled card that Alec had given her. She showed it to Mr Harris.

'This man's been up at Stephanie House. He says he'd be interested in buying the house if we ever want to move.'

'Move!' said Mr Harris. 'But you've only just arrived!' Then he turned the card over and looked at the name. 'Oh,' he said, 'I know him. He was the fellow who came to see me about Stephanie House. He was interested in its history too. He said his family used to live round here.'

'Do you know anything about the family. Do you know where they lived or what they did?' Claire tried to make the question sound casual.

Mr Harris rubbed his chin and frowned. 'No, not much. He said his great grandfather had been a builder and had had some connection with Stephanie House. Jeremy Knight seemed to think the old man had a secret passion for the beautiful Mrs Finbow.' Mr Harris laughed and pushed the pony's nose away from his pocket. 'But then,' he went on, 'if her portrait's anything to go by, most of the men in the district were probably secretly in love with her.'

'Who gave the portrait to the museum?' asked Claire.

Laura went on brushing the pony, but she was listening hard.

'I can't help you there, I'm afraid,' said Mr Harris. 'I expect I could find out easily enough, but I don't know much about the portrait. It isn't normally on display; I just dug it out from the archives along with the other stuff about Stephanie House.'

He looked at his watch. 'Well, I must get back. I've got a meeting in half-an-hour. I tell you what,' he added. 'You could come to the museum with me and do some of your own research if you like.'

Claire nodded. 'I'd like that,' she said, 'Can Laura come too?'

Mr Harris led them down into the museum basement and got out a big box file from a cupboard.

'Some of the stuff in here is what I showed you and your dad,' he said. 'I just picked out the most interesting things. But you may come across more information about the house.' He paused. 'Jeremy Knight spent some time down here. You could ask him if he's found out any more.'

No fear! thought Claire, as she knelt down on the floor and opened the box, but aloud she said, 'Thanks a lot. We'll let you know if we find anything.'

There was no natural light and the room smelt musty but the girls were soon too absorbed to notice. They looked through everything in the box, but found out nothing they didn't already know. At last, Claire got up from the floor and stretched. 'I wish I knew what we were looking for.'

'Just something to give us some clue about where the necklace might be, I suppose,' said Laura.

She picked up the miniature of Stephanie Finbow and looked at it again. 'If only she could talk!'

Claire came over and looked again at the portrait of the beautiful dark haired young woman. 'I wonder when this was painted,' she said. 'And where?'

She turned the portrait over and looked at the back, but there was no clue there.

'Surely it must say somewhere,' said Laura. Then she looked at the back more closely. 'Look, we could take this off! It's only wedged in.'

'We don't want to damage it,' said Claire nervously.

But Laura was already pulling at the velvet covered back.

'Be careful Laura!'

Little by little, she eased it out. Some of the velvet was rotten and came away with the pressure, but at last the back was off.

Inside, there was a folded sheet of paper, dotted with mildew. Gently, Laura took it out. She walked over to the electric light and started to unfold it.

'I think this may tell us when it was painted and who did it,' she said, screwing up her eyes in an effort to read the faded writing. She started to read, then she clutched at Claire: 'Look!' she whispered into the gloomy room, jabbing her finger at the crumpled paper.

Claire bent over her shoulder.

'"Stephanie Metier, Paris 1869,"' she read. Then, underneath, in a different hand, there was some other writing. It was uneven and difficult to read, as though it had been done in a hurry, under pressure. It was obviously written by someone who was not English, for the language was stilted and formal and the spelling patchy. But the message it conveyed was very clear.

It told how Stephanie Finbow was being blackmailed by Edward Knight, the builder she had secretly employed to make a safe hiding place for the necklace. How he had found out about the existence of the necklace and threatened to reveal what he knew if Stephanie didn't continue to see him and keep giving him any personal gifts he demanded from her.

She explained the reason why the necklace and the portrait, too, had to be kept out of sight. She told how her father had been a craftsman in Paris, renowned for his exceptionally beautiful settings of precious jewels. How he had been commissioned to make the necklace by a wealthy family and had shown it to Stephanie before it went to its owners. She had fallen in love with it and persuaded her father to let her have her portrait painted wearing the necklace. Against his better judgement, he agreed and the portrait was painted. But the more she wore it, the more Stephanie became obsessed with the necklace and determined, somehow, to possess it.

By this time, she had met Jocelyn Finbow and knew she was going to leave Paris. So, when the necklace was due to be delivered to its owners by her father's servant, Stephanie managed to substitute another package, containing some worthless trinket.

By dropping a word here, a hint there, she had let it be known, in the market, among the kitchen staff, anywhere, in fact, where unscrupulous ears might hear, that, on a certain day, her father's servant would be carrying something very valuable through the streets of Paris.

She hadn't really expected her plot to work, and, if it hadn't, she had devised a clever story as to how the packages had got mixed up. However, to her surprise, the plan worked all too well and the servant was robbed on his way to deliver what he thought was the priceless necklace. Up until then, it had all been a rather unreal game to Stephanie, but suddenly it was a game no longer and the necklace was hers.

Shortly after this, she disappeared to England and no one ever guessed that she had stolen the necklace. No one, that is, except Edward Knight, the builder.

Right at the end there were a couple of desperate sentences, saying how Stephanie regretted her foolish actions, how the necklace had brought her nothing but unhappiness and that now she had only the portrait to give Edward Knight; it was the last of her personal belongings and she was terrified of what he would do next. This was why she was making this confession, in the hope that someone, some day might find it and understand.

The girls read it with increasing amazement. When they'd finished they stared at each other. Claire let out a long breath. At last there was some proper evidence of the existence of the necklace! At last the dreams were making sense!

Laura carefully refolded the paper and replaced it, then she eased the velvet covered back of the portrait into place.

'Wow!' she said. 'No wonder she wanted it hidden!'

Claire turned away and walked back and forth from the cupboard to the stairs. Even though they knew the necklace did exist, they weren't much further forward. She frowned and chewed at her fingernail.

'But she never says *where* it was hidden! It's so frustrating! We know why it was hidden, but we've no idea where.'

'I suppose only Edward Knight and Stephanie ever knew,' said Laura.

Claire went up to Laura and took the portrait from her. She turned it over and over in her hands. 'And now perhaps Jeremy Knight knows, too,' she said. 'He told your dad that his great-grandfather had been a builder and had some connection with Stephanie House, didn't he?'

Laura nodded. 'Edward Knight must have been Jeremy's great-grandfather. It all fits.'

'And somehow,' said Claire, who had continued to pace up and down, 'somehow, Jeremy has just found out about the necklace and the fact that it's hidden at Stephanie House.' She continued to chew at her finger-nail, concentrating hard, trying to figure out how he could know. 'Maybe he came across some old family letter or something and put two and two together . . .'

'Umm, maybe,' said Laura, but she wasn't really listening. She was into the box again, searching for something else. Methodically, she went through every document.

'What are you looking for?' asked Claire, squatting down beside her.

'There must be *some* record of who gave the portrait to the museum,' said Laura, squinting at one piece of paper after another.

'Does it matter now . . .' began Claire, but she was interrupted.

'Here. At last! Here it is!'

Laura waved a piece of paper at Claire. It was a dull-looking letter from the County Council and it had been written only a few years ago.

'No wonder we missed it! It looks so ordinary.'

Together they read the letter. It was to the previous curator of the museum telling him that the portrait had been unearthed at the council offices and that it had originally been bequeathed to the town by a local builder, Edward Knight, on his death in 1906. The Council officers now felt that the museum should have it.

Claire looked again at the portrait in her hands. 'Enamelled gold, set with rose and brilliant-cut diamonds, rubies, emeralds, pearls and a sapphire.'

'We'll have to tell someone about all this,' said Laura, and Claire nodded. They couldn't keep it to themselves any longer.

In silence, they packed up all the papers and put them carefully back in the box. Then they laid Stephanie Finbow's portrait gently on top and put the box back in the cupboard.

They walked up the steps from the basement and into the main part of the museum. In the hushed atmosphere, their footsteps were loud on the polished floor.

When they reached Mr Harris's office, Laura went inside. 'I'll go and see if Dad's ready to go home yet.'

Claire hovered outside the door where Mr Harris's secretary was piling up books which had been strewn on her desk. She smiled at Claire, recognising her.

'Everyone seems very interested in your house these days,' she said as she picked up one book that lay open and started to smooth back a turned-down page.

'Really?'

'Yes,' she went on, 'We had that other gentleman here again this afternoon. He was looking through all these reference books.'

Claire clenched her hands. 'Jeremy Knight again!' She swallowed and tried to keep her voice even. 'Did he find anything interesting?'

'I don't know. But he left a bit of a mess to clear up!'

'Let me help you,' said Claire. She had seen the turned-down page and she took the book from the secretary's hands. Before closing it, she glanced quickly at a short paragraph which had been lightly marked with a pencil.

'. . . there is a contemporary reference to a matching necklace, but this was apparently stolen and has never come to light. It was described as follows: enamalled gold, set with rose and brilliant-cut diamonds, rubies, emeralds, pearls and a sapphire.'

Her heart hammered in her chest. It was the description that had been in her head all this time! All these past weeks, those words had burnt into her brain and they had been right! But now Jeremy Knight knew everything about the necklace, too.

She read on. All the dates fitted. The missing necklace would have been very valuable; it was European and a pair of priceless earrings which matched the necklace were now in a London museum.

She closed the book, noting its title, then picked up some others and followed Mr Harris's secretary to some bookshelves at the far end of the corridor. Coming back, she noticed a man on his way down to the basement. He stared at Claire for a moment before continuing down the stairs.

It was Jeremy Knight.

## Chapter Eight

They'd hoped to tell Mr Harris about the necklace on the journey home, but he had a colleague with him and as soon as they reached the house, the two men disappeared into Mr Harris's study.

'We must tell Mum and Dad,' said Laura.

'Yes,' Claire agreed. 'I wish we'd brought that letter back with us, then we could show it to them.'

'At least we can tell them about it.'

'OK.'

But there never seemed to be a convenient moment. Mr Harris was deep in conversation with his colleague and Mrs Harris was busy cooking in the kitchen while Tim and a friend roared in and out, banging doors and shouting with laughter.

Just when Claire and Laura thought there was at last an opportunity to tell them, the doorbell rang and Claire's Dad arrived, so there was more chat and laughter. Then Mrs Harris insisted that they all stayed for supper and soon the girls were part of a cheerfully noisy meal.

They'd hardly finished eating before it was time to go and visit Mum in hospital, so Dad picked up Claire's things and bundled her and the dog into the car.

'We'll get the letter in the morning,' whispered Laura, as Claire left. 'I'll go to the museum with my Dad, and you get your Dad to drop you off on his way to work. Once we've got the letter, they'll have to believe us.'

Claire nodded. 'OK,' she whispered. 'I'll see you at the museum in the morning.'

As they drove away, Claire told Dad about the riding and their visit to the museum. She started to try and tell him about the necklace and the letter but, although he grunted his reactions to her chat, Claire knew that he wasn't really paying attention. Underneath his cheerfulness, he was worried. Worried about Mum and worried about the factory too. Claire changed the subject. 'Are things any better at work, Dad?'

Dad glanced at her sharply. 'What do you mean?'

Claire looked down at her hands and blushed into the twilight. 'I'm sorry. I overheard you and Mum talking the other night. I know all about the rumours and the money problems and everything.' She hesitated. 'I'm sorry – I didn't meant to eavesdrop . . .'

Dad said nothing for a while as he negotiated the bends in the country roads. Then he put out his free hand and patted Claire's knee.

'I'm glad you know, love,' he said quietly. 'It will be good to talk to someone about it. I don't want to upset Mum any more at the moment.'

'Is it bad, then?'

Dad nodded. 'I know I can get that factory going, Claire. The town needs it and there are men who have always worked there who know nothing else. They would all have to move away if the factory closed down. It would be good for everyone if I could get it functioning properly.'

'But you need money?' said Claire.

'Yes. I need a lot of money.' He cleared his throat. 'When Mum and I first came down here to look at the factory, everyone was so helpful and friendly. The bank seemed happy to lend money, all the local suppliers said they'd give me credit. Now, almost overnight, that's all changed.'

'Bad luck house,' thought Claire, and aloud, she said, 'Is it because of these rumours?'

'Yes. I think it must be. Somehow, this story has got round that I'm going to close the factory down and use the land to build a whole lot of holiday homes.'

'Local people would hate that!'

'Yes, of course they would. That's probably why all these doors are suddenly shutting in my face; people don't trust me any more. They don't believe I'm even going to try and get the place on its feet again.'

'And you still don't know who started these rumours?'

'No. I've no idea. If I had, I could tackle the person face to face.'

Claire sat silently in the passenger seat. *She* knew. She was absolutely certain who it was. But she couldn't prove anything. Not yet.

They drove through the town and out the other side onto the road that led to the hospital. Dad drummed his fingers on the steering wheel. Suddenly he laughed.

'What's the matter?'

'Some man came to the office today and offered to buy Stephanie House!'

Claire suddenly felt cold. She sat very still.

Jeremy Knight! Her mouth was dry and she swallowed. 'You wouldn't Dad, would you? Sell the house, I mean?' Her voice was husky.

Dad laughed again. 'No, of course not. We've only just bought it.' He went on. 'Apparently this fellow saw Stephanie House was for sale but he was too late – we'd already bought it. He said if I ever wanted to sell it, he'd give me a good price.'

I bet he did! thought Claire, but she said nothing.

'A very good price. Much more than we paid for it. He's obviously well off because he wants a house in the country as well as his place in London. 'And,' went on Dad, 'he's got the cash. There'd be no waiting.'

Claire dug her nails into the upholstery of her seat. 'You wouldn't ever sell it though, would you, Dad?' she repeated.

'No, of *course* not. Well . . . not unless things got really bad.'

Claire looked out of the window. The countryside was very beautiful in the summer twilight. Jeremy Knight is biding his time, she thought. Spreading rumours about Dad so that he'll be ruined and have to sell the house and move away. He thinks he can afford to wait because no one else knows about the necklace.

Aloud, she said, 'I know who came to see you. His name's Jeremy Knight, isn't it? He was up at the house today.'

'Yes. Yes, that's right. I expect Alec told you.'

They didn't speak for the rest of the journey, and soon Dad swung the car into the hospital carpark. As they walked towards the building, Dad said, 'Don't say anything to Mum about the factory. I don't want her worrying.'

Claire promised, but she knew it would make no difference. Mum always knew if something was wrong. She had a nose for it!

Mum was dressed and sitting by her bed writing letters when they arrived. She stood up and hugged them in turn.

'Oh it's lovely to see you,' she said. 'I'm so bored sitting here doing nothing all day when there's such a lot to do at the house.'

'Don't even think about the house,' said Dad firmly. 'Just sit here and get fatter.'

Mum made a face, then she asked, 'How's everything at work?'

Claire looked at Dad. 'Oh, not bad,' he said quickly, but Mum knew him too well.

'Nothing's changed then?'

Dad scratched his ear and looked embarrassed. 'Well, no, not really.'

Mum's eyes blazed. When she had not been worrying about the baby, she'd thought constantly about the situation at the factory. She seemed to forget that Claire was there and was supposed not to know what had happened. 'Have you spoken to all the staff yet?'

'No, I've been too busy, I . . .'

'Then you *must*! If you leave it any longer it will be too late. Promise me you'll do it tomorrow. Talk to them all. Take them into your confidence. That's the only way to get them to trust you and to stop these vicious rumours.'

Claire had never seen her mother so angry; her face was flushed and she was gripping tightly onto Dad's arm. '*Promise* me!' she said again, shaking him to get a reaction.

Dad looked pale and tired and Claire knew why her Mum was so angry. She was determined that no stupid rumours should stop all that Dad wanted to do for the factory – and for the town. It would destroy him if he had to admit defeat.

'All right,' he said at last. 'I promise.'

Mum's face relaxed and she sat down again and became her normal self, asking Claire about her day, about the riding lesson and the trip to and from Stephanie House to fetch the dog.

As she was describing her day, the events in the museum came flooding back and suddenly, Claire felt she would burst if she didn't tell her parents about the necklace. She couldn't keep it to herself any longer and the story all came out in a great rush, words tumbling over one another, everything muddled up in her excitement.

'Hold on!' laughed Mum. 'I can't understand a word! Take it calmly!'

So, she tried to explain about the necklace, the portrait, her dreams, the letter and, lastly, about the threat from Jeremy Knight.

But, to her amazement, her parents didn't seem to take it seriously. She got more and more upset, until at last, Dad said, 'Now look love. I can see you and Laura are excited about what you've found out, but you're jumping to conclusions.'

'What do you mean?' said Claire, cross that they didn't seem to believe her.

'I mean that you've got no real reason to believe that the necklace is still hidden in Stephanie House. If it ever was, then I expect someone found it years ago.'

'But what about Jeremy Knight?'

'Your imagination's working overtime, love,' said Mum. 'He's probably quite genuine. I expect he fell in love with Stephanie House, too, just as we did, and he wants to find out more about it.'

'He may be an expert on old houses for all we know,' put in Dad.

'But the jewellery books . . .'

'He's a jeweller, Claire. He's interested in jewellery.'

Claire fell silent. How could they doubt her? How could they think that Jeremy Knight was just an innocent stranger who happened to be interested in jewellery and old houses? She *knew* she was right. He was evil. He wanted that necklace and he was prepared to destroy Dad so that he could get it.

'But can't you *see*!' she said, in desperation. 'He's the person who's spreading all these rumours about you, Dad. He wants us out of the house so that he can take it apart brick by brick, if necessary, until he finds the necklace.'

Her parents looked at each other and a startled expression passed between them. Then Mum said gently, 'What you need is a good night's sleep.'

It was dark by the time they got back to Stephanie House, and Claire was so tired and stiff that she could hardly stumble up the stairs to bed. Before long, she had drifted into the deep sleep of exhaustion.

The dream she had that night was frighteningly vivid. Francis Finbow was there again, more real and more urgent than ever before, the necklace in his hand sharply in focus. This time, though, he wasn't in the usual place beside the river, but in the bedroom. At first, Claire didn't recognise the room because it was differently furnished, but as the image became clearer and clearer, she made out the window and the seat below it and, beside the window, the shadowy figure of Stephanie, her beautiful face turned towards Claire in a silent plea.

'But where *is* it?' shouted Claire in her dream, tossing and turning in her bed.

Then she woke up, trembling, the dream still with her in all its intensity.

Her eyes were heavy-lidded with fatigue, but she switched on her bedside light and dragged herself out of bed, standing on the bare floorboards, hugging her arms and shivering. She was aware that the dog was awake, too, and alert. He came over to her and absently she pulled his ears. Then, as she felt the warmth of his body beside her, she remembered something. Last time she'd dreamt of Francis, the dog had whined and fussed and dug frantically at the rug in the middle of the room. She forced herself to think clearly. Where exactly had he dug? Had *he* been trying to tell her something – give her a sign? How *stupid* she'd been not to realise! She knelt down beside the dog and whispered in his ear, 'Find it, boy. Show me again!'

The dog whined softly but didn't move. Claire frowned, then she said urgently, 'Francis!'

He stiffened immediately and his head jerked up. Then he walked over to the middle of the room and started to dig at the rug in exactly the same spot as before.

Claire put her hands to her head. It was *here*. It had been here in her bedroom all the time!

She patted the dog and spoke to him calmly. 'All right, boy. You can stop now. I understand.'

Carefully, she rolled back the rug and saw nothing but unyielding floorboards. She sat back on her heels and thought. She'd need Dad's tool box; she'd make a lot of noise and she'd certainly wake him up and he'd never agree to her demolishing half her bedroom floor just because of some wild idea. At least, that's how he'd see it.

Slowly, Claire replaced the rug and climbed back into bed, calm in the certainty that she knew, at last, where Stephanie had hidden the necklace. She would come back here in the morning, just as soon as she and Laura had the letter from behind the portrait at the museum. They'd have time, then, to take up the floorboards and look properly. No one would be around to ask awkward questions. Lizzie wasn't coming to the house tomorrow and nor was Alec; it was their shopping day.

Claire smiled to herself. At last they were getting somewhere! She crawled back into bed and was soon deep in a dreamless sleep.

## Chapter Nine

The next morning, Dad drove Claire to the museum on his way to work. As they sat waiting for the traffic lights in the High Street to change, Claire said, 'Are you going to talk to all the people at the factory today?'

Dad smiled at her. 'You're worse than your mother! Yes, I will. Though whether it will do any good . . .'

'It's worth a try.'

'Umm, I suppose anything's worth a try,' he said, but there was little conviction in his voice.

He gave Claire a goodbye kiss as they stopped outside the museum.

'Be careful, love,' he said, frowning.

He sounded serious, and Claire looked at him. 'What do you mean?'

'I don't want you and Laura involved in anything unpleasant.'

'You mean Jeremy Knight?'

Dad looked awkward. 'I don't suppose there's anything in all this,' he said. 'But if you *do* find out more about him, then I want you to tell me, right away. OK?'

A wave of relief swept over Claire. He *did* suspect Jeremy Knight after all! And, once they'd got the letter . . .'

She smiled her reply. 'OK Dad, I promise.'

She and the dog got out and she waved as the car rejoined the morning traffic in the High Street.

'Good luck with the talk!' she shouted, and Dad raised a hand in acknowledgement.

'Wish me luck, too,' she murmured. If she was right, it shouldn't be long before they found the necklace and then, at last, the house would be the peaceful place it had been before, before Stephanie Finbow's guilt and remorse had affected the atmosphere and earned it the name of 'bad luck house'.

Laura was already at the museum, and together they went round the back of the building to a place where they could leave the dog.

As soon as she was sure they couldn't be overheard, Claire said, 'I know where the necklace is hidden!'

Laura stopped in her tracks, her eyes wide. 'What! Where! How did you find out! Quick, tell me!'

So Claire told her about last night's dream and how the dog had tried to show her where the necklace was hidden.

Laura frowned. 'Are you sure?'

'Quite sure. We must go back as soon as we can and take up the floorboards. It's under there somewhere, Laura, I know it is.'

'But . . .' Laura started.

'Just *believe* me,' said Claire gently, and Laura said no more.

They settled the dog in the caretaker's office then went down to the museum basement once more. They took the box out of the cupboard and carefully removed the lid. Laura frowned. 'I thought we'd left the portrait right on top she said.

'We did.'

Laura shrugged. 'Oh well, it must have slipped. It's down the side now.'

Claire looked, and immediately felt uneasy. Instinctively, she glanced behind her, but there was nobody else in the room. She shivered and wished they were outside again in the sunlight and fresh air.

'Come on Laura. Let's get the letter and go back to Stephanie House.'

'All right, all right,' said Laura, as, once more, she eased the back off the portrait. 'But we won't go straight to Stephanie House,' she added, 'I want you to come home with me first. I've got a surprise for you.'

'But we must find the necklace! Can't the surprise wait?'

'No,' said Laura, smiling, 'It can't.'

The back came off the portrait more easily this time, and Laura looked for the mildewed letter. She frowned, then looked on the floor. 'That's funny,' she said. 'It must have fallen out.'

Claire shook her head and once again glanced about the musty room. She suddenly felt very frightened. 'Nothing fell out,' she said slowly. 'And we put the portrait back yesterday exactly where we'd found it.'

Laura stared at her. 'Then what . . .?'

Claire continued. 'Jeremy Knight was here yesterday,' she said. 'Don't you remember? I told you. I saw him when I found the description of the necklace in the book.'

Laura nodded. 'And you think . . .?'

'I'm sure of it. He was here in the basement yesterday after we'd been here and he saw that we'd tampered with the portrait. He must have taken the back off himself, found the letter and removed it. Now he's got the only piece of evidence that could possibly connect him with Stephanie Finbow's secret.'

Laura continued to stare for a moment with the two halves of the picture frame in her hands. She said nothing more but she replaced the back on the portrait with deliberate care. Then she started to look in the box again.

'I wonder if the Council's letter's still here?'

'That doesn't matter so much . . .' began Claire, but Laura interrupted her.

'That's gone, too.'

She sat back on her heels, realising for the first time, what this meant. 'Then, he knows that we suspect him? He knows we found that letter before he did.'

Claire nodded and the girls looked at each other.

'He won't waste time, now,' said Claire. He'll get into the house somehow and try and find the necklace. We must get there and find it before he does!'

'Let's tell Dad,' said Laura. 'I'm scared.' Then she remembered. 'Oh no, he's gone to some meeting miles away. He said we'd have to go back home on the bus.'

Claire put the lid back on the box and heaved it into the cupboard. 'Come on, then,' she said, pulling at Laura's sleeve. 'Let's go and catch the bus.'

'OK, I'm coming! But the bus doesn't go past Stephanie House, and we can get there quicker if we go back to my home first. Anyway,' she added, 'I think we should tell Mum what's happening. Perhaps she could come with us.'

Claire chewed at her nails. 'All right. But let's hurry.'

They had a difficult journey back. At first, the driver refused to let the dog on the bus and was about to drive off and leave the girls to walk, when Claire burst into tears of rage and frustration. To avoid an embarrassing scene, the driver finally relented and let them on, but he scowled at them as he took their money. Then, because Claire's mind was racing ahead to Stephanie House and the necklace and Jeremy Knight, she didn't listen to what Laura was saying and, for the first time, they nearly quarrelled.

'You might be a bit more excited about this surprise I've got for you!' said Laura crossly.

With difficulty, Claire concentrated on what Laura

was saying. 'I'm sorry! I'm so scared we'll be too late – that Jeremy Knight will get there before us. I can't think of anything else.'

At last they reached Laura's house. The driver was still muttering darkly about animals on public transport as they got off the bus and ran up the lane. Still running, Laura went round to the back door of the house, then she stopped short when she realised it was locked. She turned to face Claire and the dog who arrived, breathless, behind her. 'Oh *no*! I forgot. Mum's taken Tim to the dentist. She told me. She won't be back until midday.'

'We can't wait that long,' said Claire. 'We'll have to go to Stephanie House on our own.'

'But surely the doors are locked. Jeremy Knight won't break in will he?' Laura looked scared. She didn't want to go to Stephanie House now. It would have been different if Mum or Dad had been with them. Oh *why* were grown-ups never there when you needed them!

Claire shook her head. 'A few locked doors aren't going to stop Jeremy Knight.' She moved slightly to put her hand through Laura's arm. 'Please come with me, Laura. I don't want to go on my own, but if I have to, I will. I know if I don't get that necklace, Stephanie House will always bring bad luck to the people who live there.'

For a moment, Laura hesitated, then she squeezed Claire's hand. 'All right. If you really think it's that important, I'll come.'

Claire gave a sigh of relief. 'Thanks,' she said. 'Let's go and get the bikes.'

'Not so fast,' said Laura. 'Remember, I told you I had a surprise for you.'

'Yes, but not *now* . . .'

'Yes, *now*,' said Laura firmly. 'Close your eyes and give me your hand.'

Claire frowned with impatience, but she did as she was told.

Laura led her into the stable. 'OK, you can open them now.'

Claire opened her eyes and for a moment she could see nothing in the cool, dark stable except specks of dust as they danced down a shaft of sunlight which came through the open door. Then, as she became accustomed to the gloom, she saw at last the surprise that Laura had been talking about.

Both stalls in the stable were occupied! Laura's pony was in one and in the other stood a grey mare with a pretty head and a gentle eye.

'Who does she belong to?' asked Claire, going up to the pony and fondling her mane. 'She's lovely.'

'She arrived last night after you'd left. I'm looking after her for a friend for a couple of weeks while they're away on holiday,' said Laura. 'I promised to exercise her.'

'Oh,' said Claire, feeling vaguely disappointed.

'So,' went on Laura, smiling, 'You can have my pony and I'll take this one. We can ride out together!'

For the first time that day, Claire's face lit up.

'No more bumpy biking!' she said, grinning. Then, 'Can we go out now, right away?'

'To Stephanie House?' said Laura, 'Sure. Just as soon as we saddle up and I find you some jodhpurs.' And then another thought struck her. 'I'd better leave a note on the back door, so Mum knows where we've gone.'

Claire was so anxious to reach Stephanie House that she didn't even try to hold in the pony as they followed behind Laura and the grey. They galloped along the track by the river, and the dog, showing its greyhound origins, streaked beside them, powerful and muscular, an instinctive racer; he didn't even pause when they passed the tree-stump where they'd seen Francis. When they reached the hill leading up to Stephanie House, they slowed down and let the ponies walk for a few minutes before the steep climb.

'What are we going to do when we get there?' asked Laura.

Claire had it all worked out. 'We'll get Dad's tool box from the garage and we'll go up to my room and set to work on the floorboards.'

Laura looked up at the sky. The sun had gone in and a bank of clouds was already building up fast. Secretly she still doubted they'd find anything at all under the floorboards in Claire's room and, if they didn't, she wondered how long Claire would persevere and how much damage they would do. It might all take a very long time, and she didn't want to ride home in a storm.

'Will it take long?' she asked.

Claire shook her head. 'It shouldn't, not if the necklace is where I think it is.'

Still avoiding Claire's eyes, Laura said, 'What shall we do if Jeremy Knight is already there?'

Claire swallowed. She hadn't allowed herself to think too deeply about this possibility. 'We'll have to face that when it happens,' she said shortly, and urged the pony on.

They dismounted and went into the back garden through the gate. As Laura unsaddled the ponies, put on their headcollars and tied them up, Claire crept round to the front. The place was deserted. She ran back to Laura. 'Jeremy Knight's not here!' She grinned, took off her riding hat and ran her hand through her hair.

Her relief was so obvious that Laura smiled. 'OK then,' she said, 'we'd better get on with this carpentry job!'

They got the tool-box from the garage and heaved it to the front door. Claire fumbled in the pocket of her jacket, found the key and put it in the lock. Then, as she tried to turn it, she frowned, and the panic she had felt in the museum gripped her again. Her heart started to beat faster and there was a nervous knot in her stomach. Slowly she removed the key. It wasn't needed because the door was already open.

The girls looked at each other. Fighting back her fear, Claire pulled a face and said, as casually as she could, 'Dad probably forgot to lock up this morning.' But it wasn't true; she'd watched him turn the key in the lock that morning as she sat in the car waiting for him to drive her to the museum. She glanced sideways at Laura who seemed to have accepted the explanation, and they crossed the front hall in silence and mounted the beautiful staircase, holding the tool-box between them. Claire was conscious of every sound they made and her eyes darted this way and that but she saw no one.

The dog bounded ahead of them and went straight into Claire's bedroom. They followed him, pausing instinctively at the door to confront the atmosphere inside.

'Can you still feel it?' asked Claire.

Laura shivered. 'Yes. Even more so. It seems to be much stronger now.'

Claire only nodded, but she thought she knew why the feeling was so strong. Jeremy Knight was near; perhaps he had already been in the house. In any case, he was a threat and his presence was deeply disturbing to Stephanie House. Of that there was no possible doubt.

Once inside the bedroom, Claire shut the door behind them and then rolled back the rug, exposing the bare floorboards. They looked smooth and unyielding and, for a moment, she had her doubts. Was the necklace really under there? Then she felt a wet nose thrusting into her neck as she squatted on the floor; beside her, the dog started to whine quietly and, once more, she felt certain she was right, just as she had last night after the dream.

Laura peered at the floorboards. 'They're all screwed down and some of the screws are really rusty; it's going to be hard to undo them.'

Claire said nothing, but she took a screwdriver out of the tool-box and started work. Holding the screwdriver, she allowed herself a quick smile as she remembered Dad, wrestling with the kitchen shelves.

'How do you know it's the right floorboard?'

'I told you! It was where the dog was standing – both times!'

'But the dog was on the rug, wasn't it?'

Claire bit back her anger and said patiently, 'Yes, but I marked the floorboard underneath. Look,' and she pointed at a faint biro mark on the wood.

'Oh.'

Laura rummaged in the tool-box and found another screwdriver and attacked the rusty screw at the other end of the floorboard. They worked in silence together for a few minutes, then Claire sat back on her heels and angrily brushed her hair out of her eyes. Her face was red with effort and frustration. 'It's no good. We're never going to get them out. They're all rusted in.'

Laura stopped, too, and looked for another tool to

do the job while Claire stroked the dog and stared gloomily at the floor.

Laura held up a heavy metal spike. 'I suppose we could drive this in with a hammer at the edge of the floorboard,' she said doubtfully. 'But it would probably splinter the wood.'

'It doesn't matter what happens to the wood,' said Claire sharply. 'We want to get it up quickly, before Jeremy Knight gets here.' As she bent over to take the spike and find a hammer, she took an anxious look out of the window. But she could see nothing moving except the two ponies, shifting from leg to leg, uneasy in the mounting wind outside. Laura followed her gaze.

'There's going to be a storm soon; we shouldn't stay here much longer.'

For answer, Claire drove the spike into the side of the floorboard with all the force she could muster and the bang of hammer on metal reverberated through the house. She hit again, then bent to examine the floorboard. The spike was through, but the rest of the wood was unharmed.

'Hammer it the other way now,' said Laura, 'Then the spike will lever up the wood from underneath.'

Again and again, Claire brought the hammer down onto the spike and suddenly, just when it seemed that the wood would never yield, there was a splintering sound and an ugly jagged gap appeared in the floor.

Laura had been waiting with a claw hammer and she immediately wrenched at the gap until half the floorboard was torn away. Then Claire grabbed her torch from the bedside table and they both peered underneath.

Laura was the first to straighten up. 'There's nothing there, she said flatly.

Claire raised her head and looked at her. 'There *must* be! It's *got* to be here!'

The dog came up to them and tried to put his nose down the hole. He whined and started to dig with his paws, but the splintered wood hurt him.

Claire pushed him away and lay down. She put her arm in the hole and felt very carefully as far as she could reach under the wood. Then she withdrew her arm and sat back, confused and defeated.

Laura took the torch but still saw nothing. It was only when she was shuffling back again that something struck her as odd.

She looked again. The floorboards were screwed onto vertical pieces of wood and between all these vertical pieces of wood were gaps. Except in one place. Laura bent forward again and shone the torch. One of the gaps was filled in, and if she hadn't been looking for something unusual, she wouldn't have noticed it. She put her hand on top of the wood which filled the gap and tapped it; as she did so, the dog suddenly became very excited and pushed in beside her, making her lose her balance. She grabbed onto the wood for support and it slid smoothly open beneath her touch.

'Claire!' she whispered. 'Look!'

The wood between the gap was a skilfully crafted box with a sliding lid. The lid was now off and inside was a package done up in some old crumpled newspaper. Very carefully, the girls took out the package and, even in her excitement, Claire noted the date on the newspaper – 1871. Hardly daring to breathe, they undid it.

Neither of them would ever forget the first time they saw the necklace. 'Enamelled gold, set with rose and brilliant-cut diamonds, rubies, emeralds, pearls and a sapphire.'

Even in the darkness of the gathering storm outside, it shone with its own brilliance as it lay on the floor between them.

Claire put her finger out and touched it very gently, frightened it was still a dream and would disappear again. 'It's beautiful!' whispered Laura. But Claire could only nod; it wasn't just the beauty of the necklace, it was much more than that. Finding it meant so much more – to her, to her family and to Stephanie and Francis Finbow.

Neither of them saw the door handle turn, very slowly and very quietly, but they felt the dog stiffen beside them and they looked up.

Jeremy Knight stood framed in the doorway, looking down at the necklace.

For a moment there was silence, except for the low growling of the dog, then Jeremy Knight spoke. It was the first time they had heard his voice. It was deadly quiet and full of menace. 'That is my property,' he said. 'Give it to me at once.'

## Chapter Ten

For what seemed a long time, nobody moved, though in reality it was probably no more than a few seconds before Claire's mind unfroze and she grabbed the necklace and stuffed it, without ceremony, into her pocket. Jeremy Knight lunged towards her and at the same time there was a deep-throated growl and the dog leapt at Jeremy Knight, catching him off balance so that he fell to the floor across the doorway.

Laura looked round the room in panic. They must get out of here! But they couldn't leave by the door; Jeremy Knight blocked their way as he fought off the dog, kicking and swearing. He was stronger than the dog and it was only a matter of seconds before he'd overpower it. Then she felt Claire pushing her, away from the door towards a cupboard.

'Quick,' whispered Claire. 'Follow me.' Then, as Laura hesitated, not wanting to be trapped inside a dark cupboard, Claire gave her a desperate shove which propelled her forward and she found herself tripping, slipping, banging down a steep staircase.

They crashed into the door at the bottom and out into the kitchen.

'Come *on*!' Claire's voice was high-pitched with fear, but Laura needed no urging. Together they ran through the kitchen and out of the back door. Outside the rain lashed at their faces, but they were too frightened to care. With fumbling fingers, they untied the ponies and leapt on their backs, not even waiting to saddle them up. They paused at the back gate and lost precious seconds as Laura dismounted to undo the catch which was stiff and unyielding at the best of times but now, with the rain and her panic, it seemed it would never open. Claire glanced back.

'Hurry Laura, for goodness sake, hurry! He's in the garden. He's coming!'

And she was right. Jeremy Knight had just emerged from the back door and was running across the garden towards them. His smart shoes were spattered with mud and his suit was drenched but he was coming at them very fast.

'Oh, please *hurry*!' shrieked Claire at Laura, but the wind snatched her words away.

He'd almost reached them when, at last, Laura swung the gate open. She gave her pony a slap on the rump and it shot through, almost unseating Claire, then she ran through with the grey and vaulted on just as Jeremy Knight caught up with them. He made a grab for Laura's leg, but, on horseback, she was a match for him. She lashed at his arm with her riding crop and, in the moment when he drew back, gasping with pain and anger, she dug her heels into the grey's flanks and galloped bareback down the hill after Claire, who was slipping and sliding all over the place, hanging on, her fear and desperation giving her skill and strength she never dreamt she possessed.

If she'd not been terrified of Jeremy Knight, Claire would never had managed the ride. As it was, she clung on with grim determination gripping as hard as she could with her legs, as Laura had taught her, even though every muscle in her body complained. But the rain made everything slippery; several times, the pony skidded on the wet grass as they hurtled down the hill. Claire's hair was plastered over her face and she could see nothing in front of her. Not that it would have made much difference. With no bridle and no saddle and only a headcollar rope, she had absolutely no control over the pony and had to trust him to take her to Laura's home – and safety.

But when they reached the bottom of the hill Laura managed somehow to slew across their path and stop them in their headlong rush towards the river, and for a few seconds the girls were able to catch their breath. But the wind whipped through the willows and yesterday's calm slow river was a whirlpool. The storm made the ponies nervous and they pranced and snorted with excitement and Laura knew they wouldn't be able to hold them in for long with nothing but headcollars. She just wanted enough time to turn round and look back.

'He's gone!' she shouted triumphantly. 'We've got away!'

Claire smiled weakly, too scared to be excited and, even in her panic, feeling guilty about leaving the dog to the mercies of Jeremy Knight. 'Can you see the dog?' she asked, as she tried to sit tight while the pony jiggled beneath her.

Laura looked back again and shook her head.

Claire offered up a silent prayer for his safety and touched the bulk of the package in her pocket. The newspaper surrounding the necklace was already soggy with rain.

Then they were off again, pounding along beside the river, Laura and the grey in front and Claire, gritting her teeth and willing her muscles to obey her, flying along in their wake, her only thought to end this nightmare journey as soon as possible.

The wind and rain were relentless and Claire was bent low over the pony's neck, shielding her face from the worst of the weather, so she saw nothing in front of her and was jerked right forward when the pony suddenly slithered to a halt. They had just rounded a bend in the river and the grey had stopped, too.

And then she saw the reason why.

Coming towards them was a small figure on a bike. It was Laura's brother, Tim, his yellow oilskins billowing out as he bumped forward. When he saw them, he stopped and, cupping his hands over his mouth, he shouted. 'Mum sent me to look for you! You're to come home at once. She's worried about you.'

But the wind in the trees was loud in their ears and they couldn't hear what he said and, in any case, their eyes were not on him but on another figure, a figure who Tim couldn't see, who had just emerged from the willows behind the boy and was creeping up on him.

'Look out!' screamed Laura. But the wind snatched her warning away. She kicked the grey forward, but even as she did so, Jeremy Knight had reached Tim. With a swift, sure movement, he grabbed the boy from behind and pinned his arms, dragging him off his bike and towards the river's edge.

Claire watched, dumb with horror. Jeremy Knight must have driven back down the road, and sprinted over the field to cut them off. He'd been hiding in the willows waiting for them!

Then everything seemed to go into slow-motion. Claire's brain wouldn't react properly. She didn't know what to do or how to help. Sick with fright, she saw Laura charge towards Jeremy Knight. But this time, he was ready for her. As she came at him, he released one arm and, still holding Tim with the other, he swerved out of Laura's way and, at the same time, wrested the riding crop from her grasp. While she tried to control the pony and turn again towards them, Jeremy Knight dragged Tim nearer and nearer the river's edge. Then he stood there, his city clothes clinging to his body and the wind whipping his hair across his face. He stood and waited, knowing that the grey couldn't come close to him without risk of slithering into the river. But Laura had lost all reason. She urged the grey on and on, nearer and nearer the river until at last it reared up in fright and wheeled away. As it did so, Claire saw Jeremy Knight shout something at Laura and, although she couldn't hear what it was, she saw Laura's reaction.

The grey seemed to sense its rider's despair. It stopped prancing and stood still while Laura sat, white-faced, staring at Jeremy Knight. Then she pulled on the lead rope attached to the headcollar and walked the grey over to Claire.

Even before Laura was near enough to be heard, Claire knew what she was going to say. She could see what Jeremy Knight was up to. He was bargaining with Laura. The necklace for the boy. If Claire didn't hand over the necklace, he would throw Tim into the river. They were at the most treacherous part, the part with the deceptive current. Tim, encumbered with oilskins, wouldn't stand a chance. The bank was steep and muddy, he wasn't a particularly strong swimmer, he was terrified, and he was only nine years old.

Claire knew that she had no choice. Laura didn't even have to tell her. Slowly, she got off the pony and gave him to Laura to hold. With a heavy heart, she walked stiffly towards the river bank. She was betraying Stephanie and Francis Finbow, but what else could she do? Tim was there, struggling and terrified and she had absolutely no doubt that Jeremy Knight would carry out his threat.

Her leg muscles were weak from the strain of the ride and she was shaking with fright, but she forced herself to walk steadily onwards. When she got closer to the man and boy, she stopped and dragged the package out of her pocket. Jeremy Knight never took his eyes off her as she stood there and slowly unwrapped the layers of sodden newspaper while the rain swept over her in great mocking gusts.

At last it was revealed, in all its glory, lying in Claire's outstretched hand, defying the elements. 'Enamelled gold, set with rose and brilliant-cut diamonds, rubies, emeralds, pearls and a sapphire.'

The words burnt into her soul.

Jeremy Knight was still holding Tim tightly. Claire hesitated and took a step back. 'Let him go!' she shouted.

Jeremy Knight smiled, his eyes greedy with triumph. 'When I have the necklace,' he yelled back.

Frantically, Claire tried to think. Tim wouldn't be released until she handed over the necklace; but would Jeremy Knight let him go then? How could she know? He might keep holding him until she and Laura went away.

Whatever she did, Tim was at risk. She hesitated and turned to look at Laura for help and as she did so, a movement in the distance caught her eye. Her heart leapt with sudden hope. She must keep Jeremy Knight's attention, she must string him along, just for a few more moments.

She dropped her eyes and started to wrap up the necklace again with deliberate care, soggy fragments of newspaper coming away in her fingers as she did so.

'Give it to me!' shouted Jeremy Knight, and even the wind couldn't completely drown the fury in his voice.

Claire kept her eyes down and went on with what she was doing. She mustn't turn round. She mustn't let him see what she had seen – that pale golden shape streaking down the hill from Stephanie House, obscured now by the bend in the river as he ran at full stretch along the path. Her hands shook as she replaced the last of the paper and started, once more, towards the man and the boy, praying that her timing was right. She must keep him looking at her.

She held the package out in front of her and edged forward. Their only weapon was surprise: 'Keep looking at me, keep looking at me,' she thought.

Jeremy Knight stretched out his free hand. His fingers curled round the package, but Claire didn't let go. He pulled with more force, but only succeeded in winning a fistful of wet newspaper. He pulled again, and Claire almost lost her balance.

Then, at last, the dog was there!

Hurtling round the bend, a powerhouse of muscle, he never even slackened his speed before he flung himself at Jeremy Knight. Taken off guard, the man threw up his hands to protect his face and neck. Claire seized her chance. She pulled Tim away and together they ran over to Laura. Brother and sister managed to haul themselves onto the grey while Claire, still shaking with fatigue and fear, somehow scrambled onto Laura's pony and hung on as it followed the others, slithering round bends, splashing through puddles, homewards, away from the storm, away from danger and evil, away as quickly as they could.

They were already out of earshot when the splash came, and the only witnesses were the birds, sheltering from the storm in the bending willows.

But the moment that the ripples from the splash were overtaken by the greater power of the swirling river, so a door began to close in Claire's memory. Gradually, the images of Stephanie and Francis, which had been so vivid in her mind, faded away until they were nothing but names. It was as if she had never had the dreams or seen Stephanie by the window or Francis on the tree-stump by the river. Even the threat from Jeremy Knight suddenly began to seem unimportant. It was as though she was being urged to forget him and not to dig up the past and expose Stephanie's folly. Over and over again, the same words floated into her consciousness. 'Let it rest now. Let it rest. The necklace is safe. The necklace is safe.'

Claire was not the only one affected. By the time the children reached Laura's house, cold and wet and badly frightened, the same message had, in some strange way, transmitted itself to them all and by mutual and unspoken agreement, they said nothing about Jeremy Knight. They were all strangely silent as Mrs Harris gathered them in and dried them out and when she tried to ask questions, their replies were non-committal and quiet.

'Why did you come back on the pony, Tim? Where's your bike?'

'I fell off,' said Tim, and wouldn't be drawn further.

As they were sipping warm drinks, Mrs Harris tried again. 'It was very stupid of you to ride out in that weather bareback. What were you thinking of, Laura? And where are the saddles and bridles?'

'They're at Stephanie House,' said Claire. 'We had to leave in a hurry . . . er, we wanted to show you something.'

She caught Laura's eye and saw her nod, almost imperceptibly, in the direction of the Aga at the end of the kitchen. Claire knew what Laura meant. They couldn't keep the necklace a secret now. She got up from the table, walked over to the Aga and took her dripping jacket from the rail in front.

Everyone watched as she withdrew the sodden package from the jacket pocket and put it on the kitchen table.

There was a sudden hush in the room while Claire slowly and calmly started to unwrap the layers of newspaper. All eyes were on her and the only sound came from the wind and rain outside as the storm raged on unabated. Then, as she removed the last layer, the necklace was revealed, once again, in all its glory, and Claire stood back so that everyone could see it lying on the table, incongruous among the mugs and plates.

Then the silence was broken. Mrs Harris gasped. Even at a glance she could guess at the value of the necklace. Shocked, she scraped back her chair and stood up, her drink spilling onto the floor. 'Wherever did you get that? Who does it belong to?'

So gradually, falteringly, they told her what they could, but none of them mentioned Jeremy Knight – not even Tim who was unusually quiet and listened to what the girls had to say without interrupting. Claire and Laura didn't understand their reluctance to say anything about Jeremy Knight, but an urgent message was repeating itself in their minds. 'Leave his name out of it. Let it rest. He can't hurt you now.' And without saying anything to each other, they responded to what was a final plea from Stephanie Finbow and said nothing of his involvement, nor did they mention the letter they had found behind the portrait.

Claire felt a flood of relief wash over her. They would keep Stephanie's guilty secret to themselves. The necklace was safe now and she was calm in the certainty that Jeremy Knight could no longer harm them. It was impossible to say how she knew that he was no longer a threat, but the knowledge was deeply rooted in her mind and she was sure it was true.

'So, let me get this straight,' said Mrs Harris, at last. 'You saw the necklace on the portrait of Stephanie Finbow, then you found out about it from one of the reference books at the museum, and you say the *dog* found where it was hidden in Stephanie House!'

Claire nodded. She looked at Laura. 'Yes, he kept digging in the one spot in my bedroom and I was sure there was something underneath. So, this morning, Laura and I took up the floorboards and found the necklace.'

What a simple and straightforward explanation! It gave no indication of the panic and terror they'd experienced, the crashing down the hidden staircase, the nightmare of a ride and the threat to Tim's life.

Claire's thoughts turned to the dog. It was the dog who had first brought her to the tree-stump by the river, the dog who had shown her where the necklace was hidden, had protected them from Jeremy Knight and had even saved Tim's life.

She hoped that Mrs Harris wouldn't ask after the dog. She couldn't explain why – to Mrs Harris or to anyone else – but she knew for certain that she would never see him again. He had done his job and now he was gone. Gone from Stephanie House for ever. Gone as mysteriously as he'd arrived.

In a day or so, things had settled down. Claire wanted Laura's Dad to keep the necklace at his museum, but he insisted on taking it to the museum in London to be reunited with the matching earrings. 'You know, as its part of a special collection, they will probably want to buy it. You might get a lot of money for it.'

For a moment, Claire hesitated. If they did get any money for it, they could put it towards restoring Stephanie House. But it didn't seem right, somehow.

It had never really belonged to Stephanie Finbow; she had stolen it. And the family to whom it rightfully belonged had bequeathed the matching earrings to the museum. Surely, if that family had ever had the necklace, it, too, would have gone to the museum.

'No,' she said, at last. 'I don't think we should ask for money. It didn't belong to us, really. We just found it in the house.'

To her surprise, both Laura's parents and her own agreed with her decision. And secretly, Claire knew that Stephanie Finbow, too, would have wanted her to give the necklace and not to sell it.

The people at the London museum knew that the beautiful Stephanie Finbow was the daughter of the famous Paris craftsman, Metier, the designer of the necklace, and that she had once lived in the house where the necklace was hidden. And although it was suspected that Stephanie had had something to do with the disappearance of the necklace, nothing was ever proved and no one ever found her letter of confession.

On the day of the storm, Claire's Dad had addressed the whole workforce at the factory and, as a result, had at last secured their trust. Things were still not easy, but the tide had turned in his favour and the rumours had stopped.

A few days later, he was reading the local newspaper over breakfast and he almost choked on the piece of toast he was eating.

'Look,' he said, when he had recovered his breath, and jabbed a finger at a small paragraph at the bottom of the page.

Claire got up from the table and looked over his shoulder.

There, in black and white, was what, in the back of

her mind, she had known she would see at some time, in some form. Right from the moment they had ridden away from Jeremy Knight on the day of the storm, leaving him to the mercy of the dog, she had somehow known that he would soon be unable to harm them, that in future they would be out of his reach.

And there, in the newspaper, was a brief report of his death. She read how he had crashed his car on the day of the storm.

'Poor man,' said Dad. Then he looked at her. 'At least he won't be able to spread any more rumours about me.' Then he added, 'If it was him . . .'

'Then you *did* believe me?' said Claire. 'You did think it was him?'

Dad shrugged. 'Who knows? Perhaps. In any case, the rumours seem to have stopped now, thank goodness.'

Neither of them wanted to talk about Jeremy Knight. He had gone from their lives and they wanted to forget him.

Later that day, Claire walked down to the river and stood by the bank where the water slipped peacefully beneath the willows. Absently, she dug in the pocket of her jacket and her fingers closed round something. She drew out the crumpled and muddy business card that had first told her Jeremy Knight's name and occupation. She looked at the card for the last time then, very deliberately, she tore it into tiny pieces and dropped them into the water.

She watched as they swirled slowly round and gradually drifted downstream and out of sight.

Just before the end of the summer holidays, Claire's baby brother was born and a few days later, Dad and Claire brought Mum and the baby back to Stephanie

House. As they drove in through the gate, Granny and Alec and Lizzie Toombs appeared in the drive to greet them and they all peered into the carrycot as Dad took it out of the car.

'Isn't he lovely!'

'What a bonny baby!'

'Look at his nose. Just like his Dad's!'

Granny finally tore her gaze away from the baby.

'Have you decided on a name yet?' she asked.

Mum smiled at Claire. 'Yes,' she said.

'Well?'

'It was Claire's choice,' said Dad. 'In the end she decided for us.'

Claire went over to the carrycot and, very gently, lifted out her baby brother. Holding him close against her, she said, 'Come on Francis, I'm going to show you your home.'

*Author's note*

Although the story of Stephanie House is completely fictitious, the necklace itself does exist and can be seen at the Victoria and Albert Museum in London. It is described as follows:

'Enamelled gold, set with rose and brilliant-cut diamonds, rubies, emeralds, pearls and a sapphire. West European about 1870. Clasp 1840.'